Tales *of the* Torridge

Tales *of the* Torridge

Pauline Smith

*For Roger,
with love and best
wishes always!
Pauline*

Illustrated by Jillian Bentley
Photographs by Sue Bond

Copyright © Pauline Smith, 2015

The right of Pauline Smith to be identified as the author of this work has been asserted by her in accordance with the Copyright, Designs and Patents Act 1988.

All rights reserved. No part of this publication may be reproduced, stored in a retrieval system or transmitted in any form or by any means (electronic, mechanical, photocopying, recording or otherwise), without the prior written permission of the author.

ISBN: 978-0-9933859-5-7

Design Services: The Write Factor
www.thewritefactor.co.uk

"It takes a perverse determination to drain that instinctive curiosity away and make history seem just remote, dead and disconnected from our contemporary reality. Conversely, it just takes skilful storytelling to recharge that connection to make the past come alive in our present."

Simon Schama

To request a copy or copies of this book or for further information on stockists, please contact the author at **talesofthetorridge@gmail.com**
Orders can be shipped throughout the world.
Shipping prices available on request.

For Christopher – my rock, my compass,
my constant companion on a sea of dreams.

Contents

Introduction		1
Chapter 1	The Invader 878 AD	7
Chapter 2	The Forgotten Pioneer 1525–1584	14
Chapter 3	The Lord of the Manor 1586	39
Chapter 4	The Most Unusual Stranger 1585–1587	50
Chapter 5	The Hero of the Pestilence 1646	60
Chapter 6	The First English Dustman 1673	68
Chapter 7	The Potter's Son 1681	76
Chapter 8	The Merchant Ship Owner 1688	86
Chapter 9	The Cod Fisherman 1720	95
Chapter 10	The Dark Side	106
Acknowledgements		127
Bibliography		128

List of Illustrations

- xii   *The Torridge Estuary*
- xiii   *Street Map of Bideford*
- xiv   *The River Torridge, looking north towards Bideford, Appledore and the Estuary*
- 9   *The Vikings land on The Skern*
- 13   *The Battle of Arx Cynuit begins at Kenwith Fort*
- 15   *Stephen Borough as a young boy on Borough Farm*
- 18   *Stephen Borough watching the ships from Lookout Hill*
- 21   *Stephen Borough helps on the fishing boats in Irsha*
- 26   *Stephen Borough's first voyage to find a north-east passage to China*
- 32   *Stephen Borough's second voyage to find a north-east passage to China*
- 40   *Sir Richard and his family in Conduit Lane*
- 43   *Sir Richard Grenville aboard the Galleon Dudley*
- 49   *Ready to sail – the Galleon Dudley, the Tiger and the Roebuck*
- 55   *The Stranger arrives on Bideford Quay*
- 58   *Raleigh with the Grenvilles after his Christening*
- 62   *The Town Crier announces the death of John Strange*
- 66   *The Town Crier and his wife in Church Walk*
- 69   *Sanitary Conditions in Nunnery Walk*
- 71   *Tobacco hogsheads outside King Street warehouses*
- 75   *The Town Scavenger posts the edicts in Coldharbour*

78 *Mr. Drew watches Philip Beale fishing in the Torridge*
81 *Mr. Drew comforts Philip Beale*
85 *A hive of activity on the River Torridge*
88 *John Davie walks towards Colonial House*
90 *Lunch in Colonial House*
93 *The Bideford Merchant being loaded on the Torridge*
98 *Matthew Prust at the bottom of Cooper Street*
101 *Matthew Prust and Tommy Cox in Mill Street*
103 *Matthew Prust arrives home for Christmas*
108 *Thomas Benson as a child at Knapp House*
110 *Smuggling on Lundy Island*
© David Medcalf (photograph)
116 *Unloading* The Nightingale *in the Lundy Road*
© David Medcalf (photograph)
120 *Thomas Powe and Captain Lancey in Appledore*
123 *Marshalsea Prison, London*

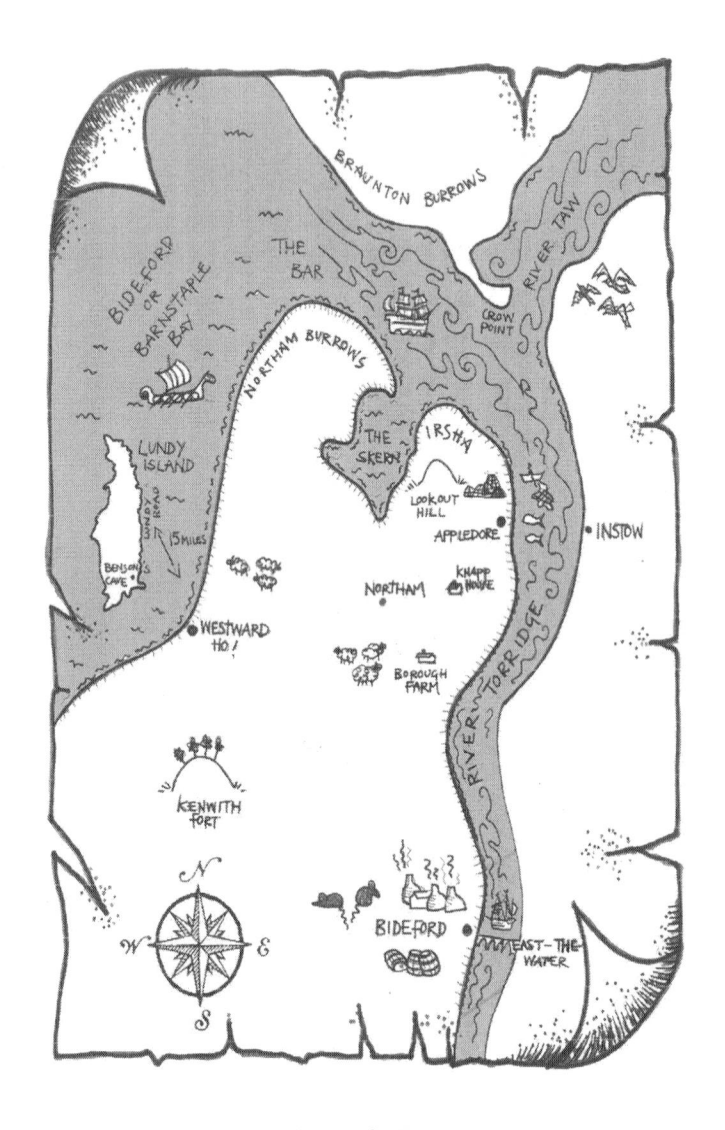

The Torridge Estuary

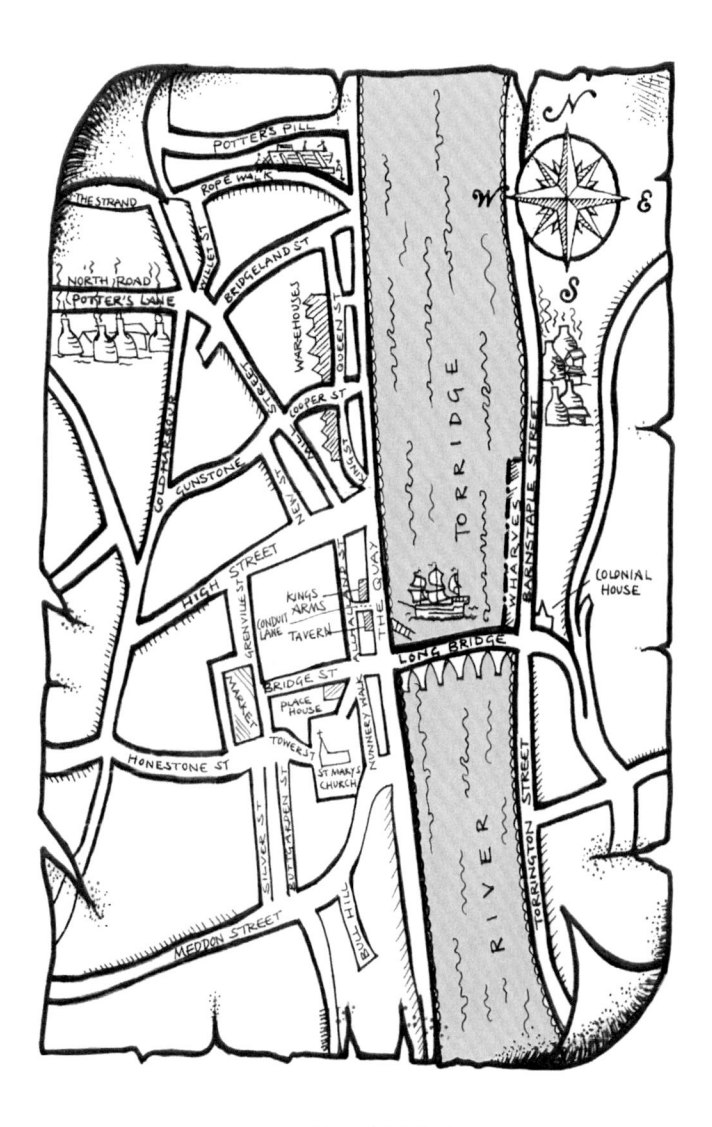

Street Map of Bideford

*The River Torridge, looking north towards Bideford,
Appledore and the Estuary*

Introduction

History is a complicated business where all manner of things conspire at certain times to affect our lives. As a child in Bideford during the 1950s and 1960s, I can remember being taught English history from textbooks as tedious and dead as the events and people they were describing. I often asked myself how the learning of it affected me, how it was relevant to me, living in Bideford. My own town seemed to have a wealth of much more interesting history. Old stone warehouses, forts, cannons, narrow, winding streets with strange names, an uneven old Bridge, tumbledown wooden shipyards dotted along the river banks, distinct yellow-glazed pottery, the long straight alley called Rope Walk. And why was the car park called The Pill? This was all history, wasn't it? The history books and the history I was surrounded by seemed to have no connection.

It wasn't until many years later that I began to understand why history had been so dull. Local historians told me stories about Torridge people who lived during some of the most significant periods of English history – the 16th, 17th and 18th centuries. Suddenly, history came alive – relevant, accessible and exciting through the images they created in my head; how and where people lived and worked on a day-to-day basis, how they relaxed, talked, worshipped, what they wore, what they ate and drank, what it sounded like and smelled like to live on the Torridge estuary during these times. The previously inaccessible framework of history was playing out at a local level in front of my eyes and these details ignited my imagination. The 'story' was back in 'history' and things were starting to fit together, to make sense. Here was context. History and I had connected.

My father used to tell me his own stories about life in Bideford during and after the Second World War. My mother's stories of the same period were about leaving industrial north Yorkshire to join the Women's Land Army in deepest Devon. All of us have stories like these, handed down through our families and friends from one generation to another. Frequently, they differ in specific detail between the different tellings. Does that matter? Not really. The essence and intent of each story live on. They cement not only our relationships but our connections to home and to a wider history.

Here I was, then, with a wealth of historical research gathered over 30 years. I also had a personal, profound knowledge of and affection for the area, but no stories to help connect its past to its present and its future. So I decided to create some of my own – stories that would offer snapshots of how it might have been around Torridge during some of the most exciting and significant periods of its history. I have tried to create narratives from my own interpretation of often-limited historical records. I hope each one will motivate a desire to find out more from what still exists. Some images and details cannot be completely verified but, in haggling about whether or not something is 100% accurate, the real sense of storytelling is lost. Some stories have a narrator, others are told by the characters themselves. Some of the characters are based on real people, some are fictional, but the events

Introduction

surrounding all of them took place on, or are claimed by, Torridge.

These are simple stories about the people of Bideford's old family, stories you can trace right back to the 16th century and, in the first, to the 9th century. They may not all be true in every detail but they are part of our heritage that otherwise run the risk of being lost in history books or, even worse, bulldozed away. If this book can awaken one person's imagination – child or adult – to sections of its under-recognised history, it will have done its job.

All of the stories, except the first, celebrate the wonderful serendipity that befell a little town in North Devon that nestles on the banks of a fast-flowing river that spills swiftly into an estuary fringed with little villages and that flows into the Atlantic Ocean. On the other side of that ocean was once an unexplored sub-continent. These historical and geographical facts provide the broader context to the book, one that can be appreciated and shared by a wide audience. Stimulating the imagination has little to do with age. Each can be read privately, read aloud in schools or at bedtime and is simple enough to be easily re-enacted. Each is designed to give pleasure to older children, grown-ups, visitors, parents and teachers in the quest for a better understanding of Torridge – a rare treasure trove of living history that has lain dormant for a long time.

Tales of the Torridge is a collection of ten stand-alone stories, illustrated with contemporary photographs upon which have been superimposed ghost-like sketches of each story's characters. They are told in chronological order, but can equally be dipped into at random. The book begins with the only story from more than 500 years ago. 1200 years ago a legend was born. That legend has captured the hearts of local people through every generation that has followed; a legend so strong that it is still remembered and argued about to this day. Some say it never took place here at all. Hubba the Dane is a Viking invader who realises the potential of the Torridge estuary as a very good place to search for the King of England, Alfred the Great, who is in hiding following his retreat to the west during the Viking invasion of Britain in 870 AD. One evening eight years later, at twilight, Hubba invades the Torridge estuary …

Next, we jump forward almost 700 years to the 16th century and a story that is seldom told about one of two brothers born in Northam. Stephen Borough was a seafaring pioneer without whose navigational achievements nothing else in the near future of Torridge could or would have succeeded in the same way. More than 400 years after he died, despite his unique achievements, Stephen tells us why part of him remains a little sad.

Much of the heritage of Torridge can be attributed to the exploits of Sir Richard Grenville, Lord of the Manor of Bideford and the town's most famous ancestor. In the third story, he has already become the first Englishman to establish an English colonial settlement in North America on Roanoke Island. Our story joins him in the spring of 1586, as he is about to return there from his home in Bideford, his ships loaded with fresh supplies. He has left a collection of English people on Roanoke, many from Bideford. The process of English settlement in North America has begun and Sir Richard's exploits will turn his home town of Bideford into the second largest tobacco importing port in England less than thirty years later. But what will he find when he returns to Roanoke?

Introduction

One of the most unusual stories of all is that of Raleigh, the Native American who came to Bideford with Sir Richard Grenville when he initially returned from Roanoke in the autumn of 1585. Although Raleigh isn't the first American Indian to come to England on an English ship, two things will happen to him in Bideford. Those two things will make him – and the town – unique in history.

Then we'll hear an announcement from the Town Crier in 1646 about the death of a brave merchant ship owner who was also Bideford's Mayor. John Strange has saved the town's life and given his own in return during the Plague. After he has made the announcement, the Crier and his wife discuss the situation on their walk home.

We will hear from Davey Heard who was the Town Scavenger in 1673. He tells us about the dreadful sanitary conditions in Bideford at that time and how regular refuse collections will shortly begin here, using empty wooden tobacco barrels as refuse bins.

The potter Thomas Beale has a son – Philip Thomas Beale. Philip's teacher, Mr. Drew, finds him out fishing in his boat on the Torridge one summer afternoon in 1681. He watches Philip and reflects on their recent conversations as Philip tries to make sense of the way his father has been treated.

We spend some time with the ship owner and merchant, John Davie, as he prepares to take lunch in his very special new house in 1688. He will be sailing shortly to his tobacco plantations on the shores of Virginia.

Matthew Prust, a Bideford fisherman, has arrived home on his ship just in time for Christmas 1720. He has been away for eight months, fishing for cod in Newfoundland.

He is trudging his weary way home to surprise his family. Along the way, he encounters some of the town's good folk.

Finally, we'll hear the terrible story of the Nightingale, a ship that belonged to the Member of Parliament for Barnstaple, who was also a ship owner and merchant trader living in Northam. What was the dreadful crime that led to the hanging of the ship's Captain? Where can you find the house from which the disaster was planned in 1752?

Stories about people like these have given Bideford its own very special history – a history you can still find, see and imagine for yourself. Here is history worth retelling, worth understanding and worth passing on.

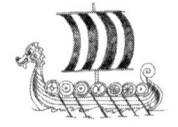

Chapter 1

The Invader
878 AD

Imagine you have three very special gifts. First, you are a human bird; you can fly. Second, you are invisible. Third, you can travel back through time, compress it and warp it to watch events that may have taken weeks in the time it takes to tell this story. Today, my invisible, time-warping bird, you have arrived back in the 9th century.

It's a clear, late afternoon in early spring and you are flying over the wild, fast-flowing river Torridge. You know it's the Torridge. You know the whole area – not just the river but the communities, the geography, the names of roads – yet everything seems so different. Face south – no buildings, no bridges, no sounds. Dense forest and tangled undergrowth trail down steep slopes and cliffs. At the bottom of these are bogs and marshes covering the banks. You stop and hover, still as the raptor you are, about thirty feet up from the oily liquid surface of the river below. Soupy little ripples slap swiftly over each other like wet clothes on a washing line.

Face north, look downriver, look towards the foothills of Exmoor. You are as still as you can be against the fierce north wind moaning and ripping up the river into your face, making salty tears stream from your bird eyes. Your bird ears scream with cold. But you can hover. And you know that, even though things are different, something else is wrong. You can feel it.

Your ears strain to catch a noise to your left. Very faint, repetitive, strange. Swoop left, soar up over the forest, follow the sound down again towards the sea, the marshes and mud flats, where the estuary joins the sea, towards the Bar.

Now the wild sea lies to the west and the tide is high. Face the sea, face the bay. Scruffy white lines of surf are beneath you, the habitual shush-shushing of surf against the shore on the Burrows. It's not that. The other noise is still there, on your right, coming and going on the wind. It's *inside* the Bar! It's in the estuary! It's coming from The Skern! Beat, Beat, Beat. Growing louder as you fly towards it. A regular drumming sound. Surely made by man? Scan … scan … scan your raptor eyes. What IS it? WHERE is it? Louder, louder, now the creak of wood and the surge of water breaking, different to surf breaking onshore. Hairs on the back of your bird neck begin to prickle.

No. This is not right. Someone is here who should not be here.

Suddenly, in the twilight, all becomes clear. Long oars are plunging into the estuary accompanied by relentless, multiple drumbeats! That is what you can hear! Those beats are conducting an orchestra of oars as they plunge into the water. Each beat says 'obey' or be killed. Long oars in long wooden boats, too many to count. You know

The Vikings land on The Skern

what these boats are, you recognise the way the occupants are dressed. Viking warriors are approaching the shore! Vikings in Northam! But why are they here? Where have they come from?

Let me tell you. These Vikings, led by Hubba and Hingwar, have crossed the Bristol Channel from South Wales. Now they have crossed the Bar, looking for your English king, Alfred the Great, here in his Kingdom of Wessex. They think he may be hiding out in the only part of England the Vikings have not already plundered since they began their invasion eight years ago ...

Turn to face south, towards Northam, the wind behind you. You must warn everyone! Then you remember – there is no Northam. Nothing except uncultivated land and hills. A few flickering flames over there? Yes, a small settlement of farmers nearby. A group of fishermen, too, on the fringe of Irsha, the dim orange glow of another small fire. But they have already heard the drumbeats and are damping down the flames. Even though you are invisible and high above the invaders, you are terrified.

Suddenly, the sound stops dead and your bird skin prickles with fear. The oars have been lifted. The Vikings are ready to land.

On the marshes around The Skern, 1200 warriors clamber off 23 boats. They pull them inland a little, struggle over the mudflats and marshland. Lights from pitch-covered torches lead their charge inland. Hideous battle cries make your wings want to fold with fear. Swarming onwards, upwards to the crest of the hill, towards Bay View Road, Cornborough Road, then left down over Pusehill towards the hill fort at Kenwith. You follow. You know Kenwith is full of Devon men and you want to warn them! But,

The Invader

of course, you can't. You're an invisible bird out of your time. All you can do is watch and follow.

Taking the fort by surprise, the Viking warriors are able to lay siege to it, hoping the Devon men will be forced out for food and water. All you can do is circle. And watch. And wait. You wait for three days …

Time moves on in a virtual flash.

Out of the deep blue of an approaching dawn, still starlit with a crescent moon, bloodcurdling battle cries are coming from the fort! Odun, the Earl of Devon, has finally issued the order to fight. The Devon men burst out and a fierce battle begins. The Devonians are brave, though badly prepared and poorly armed for such a battle. But the element of surprise is with them and they know the terrain well. The Vikings did not expect this. They are cold and drowsy with waiting. The land is inhospitable and unfamiliar. Hills and valleys make it difficult for them to know or see where they are going. The Devon men are driving them back.

The Vikings try to escape the way they came. They are desperate to get back to their ships, but they are disorientated by the unexpected fight put up by the enemy. The Vikings take flight down over the hill, towards their waiting vessels on The Skern. They reach flatter ground at last but find themselves too far inland! They need to turn left but they are trapped. And surrounded in a field on a corner between Northam and Appledore.

The defeat of the Vikings is completed at the Battle of Arx Cynuit. Most of them, including Hubba himself, are killed and their 'Raven' flag is captured by the triumphant local men. Hubba is buried in a stone tomb on the shores of the Torridge.

And so, at last, your flight of fancy is over. And imagination may be all it is or ever could have been. No one knows for sure if the Battle of Arx Cynuit took place here. Some historians believe the location to be in Beaford, Devon or Countisbury, Somerset.

But it is one possibility and the oldest story told and retold to this day in this area. It is the word Cynuit, sounding so much like Kenwith, that has led other historians to believe that this is the true location for the famous battle. Crow Point across the estuary could be a reference to the Raven standard of the Vikings. And the word Skern is Scandinavian for 'landing place'. The stone tomb, Whibblestone, was rumoured to have been located near Middle Dock in Appledore, but no remains have ever been found …

All of us have to use our imaginations to picture what might have happened, because definitive written records of this event do not exist. Yet, it is so widely believed on Torridge that, in 1890, Charles Chappell erected a memorial to the battle. You can find it on the corner of the road that joins Northam to Appledore, the corner known as Bloody Corner. In 2010, a stone memorial to the battle was constructed by a local man, Terry Bailey and engraved by local stonemason, Gabriel Hummerstone. You can find that at the west end of Irsha Street, Appledore. Members of the Hubbell Family Historical Society from various states in America visited Appledore in 2014, believing their family to be direct descendents of Hubba.

Who can say for sure? Well … you were there. You flew over the scene. You followed it. You watched it all unfold. What do you think?

The Battle of Arx Cynuit begins at Kenwith Fort

Chapter 2

The Forgotten Pioneer
1525–1584

My name is Stephen Borough. I was born in Northam on September the 25th 1525 and this is my story. It's quite a yarn really, but few people seem to know much about it around here. Given that I was the nautical pioneer who changed forever how sailors conducted their voyages, I find it a little strange. Given that I transformed how sailors explored by introducing them to navigational charts, I am more than a little downhearted. Perhaps it's because I was a peaceful, quiet man. I never fired a shot in anger and I didn't achieve the daring notoriety of others who would shortly follow me.

There is no sign of a memorial, neither plaque nor monument, to me or my brother, William, in Northam where we were born and where we lived with our family. There *is* something with our name on it, though. A housing estate, named after our home – Burrough Farm. Oh, and I almost forgot, a road – Burrough Road. I have no idea why they are spelled like that, either. It's not much, though, is it?

Stephen Borough as a young boy on Borough Farm

I was not an arrogant man, bigheaded or loud-mouthed. All I ever wanted was for my sovereign and country to profit from the skills I had to offer. I was always brought up to be God-fearing, practical, hard working and never afraid of making difficult decisions. I liked to achieve results. In my early days, not everyone could read or write and little was written down, so I imagine this might be why people have forgotten me. In my day, when a family died out or was dispersed, stories told between relatives and generations eventually faded and tended to disappear entirely. Only when a person became famous or notewothy was anything written about them. And so it was with me. My achievements *are* written down and recognised, but not here, where I was born and where I spent my childhood. I want to put my name back here, to tell you how a little boy from Northam became one of the most prominent names in maritime England.

It was a cool and blustery day when my mother Mary gave birth to me in her chamber at Borough Farm, Northam. The farm of my birth and childhood no longer exists, of course, like most of that age, even manor farms like Borough. There is still a big old stone place called Burrough House – but it was rebuilt long after my family had left the land. However, you can still find the original land where Borough Farm was situated. In fact, you can still walk along the edge of what were our fields and woodland. It belongs to your National Trust. From there it's not difficult to imagine where I played alone as a young lad, scrambling through hedges and fields with my dog to the low cliffs, then down to the Torridge below, fishing out in my little boat. I was the eldest of five but I was alone for the first eleven years of my life, before my brother, William, was born and followed thereafter by my three sisters Agnes, Margery and Jane. The farm had been in our family since 1302 and my father, Walter, worked it with his brother, my Uncle Thomas, and some local farmhands. We had a few servants in the house, too.

During my early years, I learned much about the ways of the land and the sea. From Borough, there was a fine view of Northam church, white-painted then to help sailors set their course for home and negotiate the Bar. The wind could surely blow there, coming from all directions and swirling around The Skern, up and down the estuary.

Most of all, I loved to watch the ships coming in and going out on the tides, negotiating Pulley Ridge and Crow Ridge and disappearing for a while behind Lookout Hill. Father told me they were to and from South Wales, Spain, Bordeaux and Ireland as well as the big fishing ships to and from Newfoundland. I remember how I longed to know more. I would wander around the shipyards along the edge of the river and up to Bideford sometimes, excited by the sights, sounds and smells that were to become new ships. I longed to be out on the water in them. Ships would line up at anchor in the Torridge, waiting for a favourable tide and fair weather, so they could navigate the treacherous sands and spits of the estuary and put to sea fully loaded with their cargoes.

My father Walter, my uncle John and my other uncles all had shipping interests as well as the farm to take care of. That was common back then around these parts. Unlike father and the other uncles, Uncle John Aborough was a renowned ship's Master, otherwise known as a Captain. While today, a sailor cannot become a Captain without obtaining a Master Mariner's qualification, in my Uncle

Stephen Borough watching the ships from Lookout Hill

John's day, a Master gained that title through reputation alone. My first good fortune was that Uncle John became my mentor. Although he was away at sea a lot, when he came home he would always visit us and, by the time I started school in Church Square, Northam when I was five, I could already read and write a little thanks to him. Every day I would walk down the muddy track from Borough, down Castle Street until I reached Church House. As I grew older, I realised how lucky I was that my father had allowed me to attend school. Many of my friends had to stay at home to herd the cows, clear the fields of stones or cut furze for the cloam ovens.

My teacher, Mr. Walter, helped my reading and writing to come on a treat. Some said my handwriting was the best they had ever seen and I had started number work, too, using an abacus. From the schoolroom, it was only a mile or so down to Irsha and then to Appledore and I would venture there with my friends whenever time allowed. As time went on, I found myself drawn there more and more frequently, scrambling on and off the little fishing boats, barefoot, helping to mend nets and whatever other tasks the men there required. I had relations down there, too, and they showed me how to handle a fishing boat. It was quite a skill in the fast tidal waters of the estuary.

My! What problems that Bar caused. Shipwrecker Bar we called it, being as it was full of hazards. So many ridges to negotiate! They used to say if you could sail the Bar, you could sail anywhere. Certainly, I was to prove them right in that respect. Anyway, the day after my 10th birthday when I had finished school, Uncle John met with me at home, having just returned from Calais.

"Well, my lad,' he did say, "'tis time for 'ee to become a man. You'm finished with school!"

Now I liked school and was a little perturbed. Yet part of me knew something big was about to happen to me and my little heart was beating like a drum.

"But, Uncle, my numbers do still need work," was all I could think of to say. "We only just started proper with them. I fear I am not yet ready … "

"Now don't you worry your head about that, Stephen. I will help you, for you will have need of figures, that's for sure. You can read and write so well as I, so you'm gwain to be a gromet for me on my ships to and fro' Calais. I have spoken with your father and 'ee's given you 'ees blessing. You'm gwain to learn what it takes to be a Master, young man. Now … what do 'ee think about that?"

Of course, what I thought of that you may only imagine! A gromet only worked on ships belonging to the Navy Royal! Gromets ranked above ship's boys but below ordinary seamen. And I knew that, because our sovereign, King Henry VIII, had fallen out with the Roman Church, the navy was getting bigger in the event of war with the Catholics. It was an exciting time for a young boy to be involved and there were good prospects, too.

Here was Uncle John fulfilling my dearest wish without the need to stay on at school a moment longer! He had just been put in charge of all the service boats to and from the Cinque Ports on the South Coast of England and the very important Staple Wool Market in Calais. The five ports – Dover, Hastings, Hythe, Romney, and Sandwich – enjoyed various trading privileges in exchange for providing the bulk of England's navy, so Uncle John had become an extremely important man. And it was into

Stephen Borough helps on the fishing boats in Irsha

this momentous period of his life that I, Stephen Borough, was being allowed. Indeed, I was a lucky Northam lad and I was beside myself with happiness. Of course, it meant moving away from mother and father, my home and the farm. But I knew the sea was where my future lay and to be a gromet was exactly what I had dreamed of, ever since I had started learning down on the slips at Irsha after school. What's more, I had expected father to send me off as a page with a well-to-do family nearby, to learn more genteel arts as a henchman – hawking or riding, hunting and shooting. I hadn't wanted that. How I looked forward to learning the skills I needed to be a gromet under Uncle John's watchful gaze. I even started to think clearly about the day when I could become a Master myself.

It wasn't very long into this new period of my life that I realised the significance of what was happening and the possibilities opening up to me. Not only was Uncle John a Master of great standing with a considerable store of sophisticated navigational instruments not always available to other Masters, but he also had strong connections with the Court in London. He was the perfect tutor for me, considered more knowledgeable in the fledgling art of navigation than most. It was a new discipline, barely acknowledged but, almost immediately, it was the study and science of navigation that intrigued me.

When I was 14, Uncle John took me on a secret voyage to Holland by order of King Henry. The king wanted us to plan and navigate a complete and safe coastal route between Sluis in Flanders and London so that he might send a fleet of ships to bring back the lady who was to become his fourth wife, Anne of Cleves. During that voyage, Uncle showed me how to plot and write a rutter (you would call it a sea route) for myself. Until quite recently, a rutter had been the only source of geographic information available to Masters and sailors. But the nautical charts that Uncle John was starting to produce, in addition to the rutters, were made possible because of the modern navigational instruments he was using. Suddenly, a Master had a visual map of the coast and the sea in front of him on a chart. This was a revolution. Uncle John taught me to use his compasses, his quadrant, his lodestone, running glass, ephemerides and charts. I was mesmerized by these new navigation techniques and I was about to plot my own chart to prominence.

Although I remained a good few years with Uncle John and joined his increasingly important naval voyages, that voyage to Flanders did more than any other to give me links to London. That was where I would steer my future as a Master. There was no going back to Borough Farm now or the slipways of Irsha. Most of Northam would have already forgotten young Stephen Borough. My family rarely saw me and I had very limited means of being able to contact them. My life now was in London. My connections and my growing renown as an up and coming Master were there, too.

Becoming a Master takes a long time. For me, it was another 13 years after that voyage to Flanders. By the age of 27, I had already been away from Borough Farm for 17 years. I had acquired a new home on the banks of the Thames, at Ratcliffe, not far downstream from the Tower of London. I had married my wife, Eleanora, and our son, Christopher, was a young boy. I had become a family man.

My first appointment was as Master of the *Edward Bonaventura*. She was the biggest of three ships chosen by a group of London merchants and gentlemen at Court, all prepared to risk funding a voyage that seemed impossible. In charge of organising it was the renowned cartographer and former Pilot Major of Spain, Mr. Sebastian Cabot. His influence on English maritime trade would soon result in the formation of the Muscovy Company – the first trading company owned by merchants rather than the Crown, transforming the trading fortunes of England throughout the Elizabethan Age and I, Stephen Borough, had been appointed one of the twelve founding counsellors. My growing navigational reputation had come to the attention of Mr. Cabot who had trusted me with the largest vessel on a voyage about which almost nothing was known in advance.

My ship carried on board the Pilot Major of the Fleet and second-in-command Richard Chancellor as well as my 17-year old brother, Ordinary Seaman William Borough. The flagship of the fleet was the *Bona Esperanza* which hosted Sir Hugh Willoughby, Captain General of the Fleet. The *Bona Confidentia*, was the smallest of the three. Now, I would wager that very few of you have heard about the expedition of 1553. Nor may you realise how fundamental it was to England at that time. The purpose of the voyage was to find a new, shorter trading route to China, through never before charted waters. Competition for trade in the Orient had become fierce and the King had been urged to find a northeast passage via the west coast of Norway through the Arctic Circle, so that England could regain her trading superiority over the Portuguese, who used to sail to the Orient around Africa, and the Spanish, who sailed there south-west via the Philippines. England badly needed its own trade routes. Trade was THE biggest word of the sixteenth century.

But a north-east passage through the Arctic? In 1553? Let me see. Just imagine for a moment that you are sailing to Norway today on a 60-foot yacht of the latest design – one of those with self-reefing sails, lots of fibreglass, navigational technology and satellite tracking, hot showers and comfortable beds. On *my* 60-foot ship of the latest design – a wooden, 3-masted sailing ship – there was no engine, no GPS, no radio, no computer, no electricity. There were no navigational charts. There were also 49 men on board. The *Edward Bonaventura* was twelve and a half feet *shorter* than the vessel in which Dame Ellen Macarthur circumnavigated the world in 2005! And Norway? That was just the beginning. After Norway, all was virtually unknown and unexplored.

This was groundbreaking exploration. It was a race, just like the race between the Americans and the Russians in the mid-1950s to put a man into space. In the end, it all came down to faith that we could do it, to prove that we were superior to other powerful nations. I was like Yuri Gagarin – the first man in space in 1961 – for I became the first man to navigate and chart the cold outer spaces of the Arctic. And I want to tell you what it was like, to try something no one else has ever attempted.

But before I begin my story, I will explain something important. In the centuries that have passed since I was alive, so much has changed – not least the names by which you refer to geographical features and places on the globe. Many of the place names that were familiar to me would mean little or nothing to you now. Therefore, I have decided to use your modern words for them, because I want you to follow my tale as clearly as possible on the maps I have provided for you.

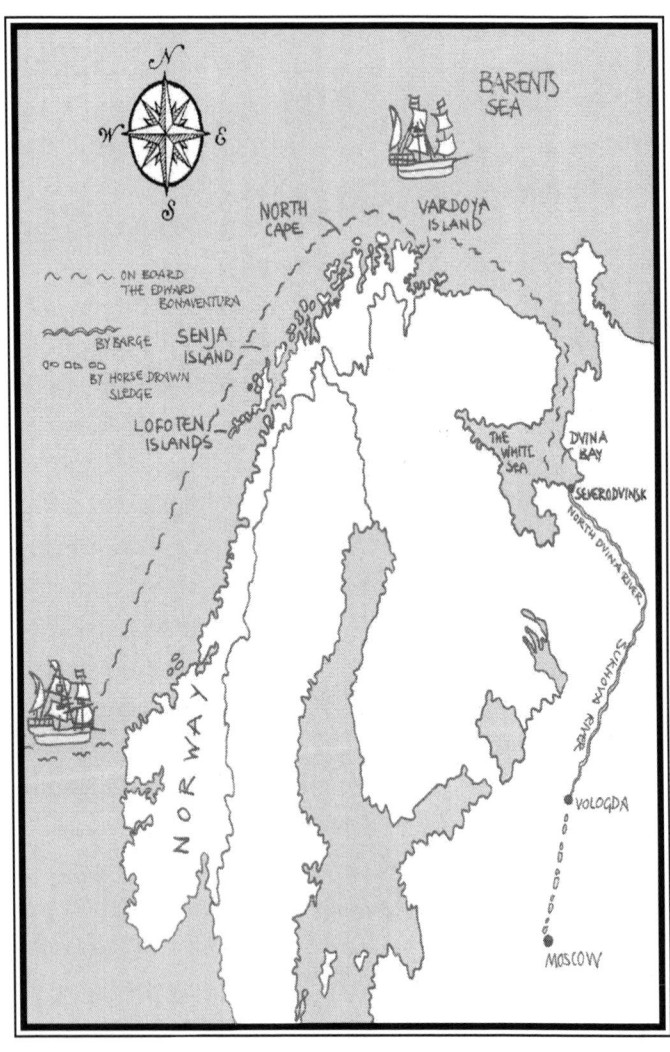

Stephen Borough's first voyage to find a north-east passage to China

We departed on May the 10th and did not return to London for another year – a year of barely credible encounters and discoveries, terrible hardships, dangers and unspeakable loss. Firstly, it took us three weeks simply to escape English waters, due to a variety of irritating trials and restraints. When we finally felt the free movement of the ships under our feet on the open sea, the sense of exhilaration for us all far outweighed any trepidation for what was to come. We had some limited sea routes, rutters, which assisted in the first part of the voyage. In the Lofoten Islands off the coast of Norway, we revictualled on July the 27th. I took great care on the way not to tell the crew about the legendary whirlpool known as the Maelstrom which was reported to be nearby. Legend had it that the Maelstrom swallowed ships whole. Mr. Chancellor and I thought it best the men were not disconcerted over something that may not exist and, as it turned out, we did not encounter it.

But we reached Lofoten later in the year than we had anticipated due to our earlier delays. Nevertheless, on July the 30th, Sir Hugh Willoughby made the decision to venture further north-east towards North Cape with the flotilla and arranged with each ship that, in the event of our ships becoming separated, we should await the arrival of the others on Vardoya Island.

Near Senja Island, at around four o'clock that afternoon, we encountered a most dreadful storm which had a voice of its own, like an orchestra of the devil. The winds roared and our rigging screamed under the pressure of it. Men were pinned down by the force of the wind or tossed around the ship, quite helpless. It was impossible to keep course and the ships were indeed separated. The last I heard were the cries of Sir Hugh. The desperation in his voice will haunt me forever.

"Mr. Borough! I beg you, sir! Please do not venture far from us!" He pleaded more than once, but I could do nothing but hold my ship steady to the best of my own ability and knowledge. We were unable to maintain contact with the others, despite his terrified voice ringing in my ears. When the storm at last abated, there was no sign of either the *Bona Esperanza* or the *Bona Confidentia*.

We were without our expedition commander.

We reached Vardoya Island and waited there one week, as agreed. There we met some Scotsmen who tried earnestly to dissuade us from pursuing our passage, but we were unable to ascertain from them a good enough reason why. When it became clear the others would not be returning, the sturdy *Edward* continued east, greatly aided by the long twilight of the days. We passed North Cape, the most northerly point of Europe, unmistakable for its 1000-foot high cliff and surrounded by low, flat tundra. In fact, I renamed it North Cape that very day. Beyond the Kola Peninsula, we finally found ourselves in a great bay which we were soon to discover was itself within an enormous enclosed sea, the White Sea. By now, we were 500 nautical miles beyond the North Cape, 500 nautical miles beyond any prior navigational knowledge.

Winter was fast approaching and we were in the uncharted waters of the Arctic. The sea around us was starting to freeze. All my experience told me that we must seek shelter in order to survive the Arctic winter. I sensed the crew's unease in this alien environment. Talk of the legendary Kraken, a sea monster of enormous proportions, was rife amongst them and the notion that one might be encountered at any time settled on the men like a gloomy fog. But, by the grace of God and their faith in me to protect them, we pulled through. As we proceeded toward a hopeful-looking bay, we came across more fishermen who were rather surprised to see their first 3-masted ship, being accustomed to their single-masted *lodias*. They spoke an unknown tongue but we learned from them, by trial and error of language and sign, that we were in Dvina Bay and, to our astonishment, that the river led inland through a vast land mass which they called Russia. Mr. Chancellor decided there was no possibility of searching further for the north-east passage to China before winter and that, instead, we should drop anchor and overwinter in Dvina Bay, near Severodvinsk.

"As safe a haven as any we shall find now, Mr. Borough," said Mr. Chancellor. "And this is what I shall do, sir. I shall explore Russia instead!"

The Governor of Dvina was somewhat afraid of Mr. Chancellor's intentions and warned him about the terrible reputation of the great Tsar, Ivan IV, whom you would know as Ivan the Terrible. Even when Mr. Chancellor tried to trade with the Governor himself, the Governor would hear none of it until we had established rights and permissions to do so from the Tsar. And, to do that, Mr. Chancellor would have to venture to the Tsar's city, Moscow.

So began what turned out to be an unexpected 600-mile journey inland for Mr. Chancellor and a small group of hand-picked men from the crew, for which they were hardly prepared in clothing, transportation or supplies. Despite his initial reservations, the Governor treated the expeditions most generously, enabling them to venture almost half-way by barge, up the Dvina and Sukhona rivers as far as Vologda. He also provided supplies and the loan of some horse-drawn sleds to complete the journey overland. As directed by the Dvina magistrates, I awaited their return with the rest of the crew on the *Edward*, in a small, sheltered bay called Unskaya Guba, some 35 miles from Severodvinsk.

The winter weeks passed quietly enough but we had no news until one day in February 1554, a messenger arrived to tell us that Mr. Chancellor and his men had returned. We sailed back forthwith to Severodvinsk.

"So, Mr. Borough, though not the one we had hoped for, it would seem that we have established a new trade route after all!"

We shared dinner that evening and Mr. Chancellor recounted his voyage, how the cold and the sheer rigidity of the terrain caused him and the crew terrible hardship. Nevertheless, he had finally reached Moscow.

"A most beautiful city, sir. A city as big as London, full of beautiful buildings. None of us knew what our reception would be from the Tsar. I found him a man of commanding stature. He was clothed in a beautiful long garment made of gold. He even wore a crown and carried a staff of crystal and gold!"

"And how were you treated, sir?" I asked.

"We were treated with generosity and good manners and the Tsar appeared fair and open to our request to trade. Upon our arrival, we were given a feast of roast swan served on golden platters. Wine was served from an enormous golden cup. After we had eaten our fill, the Tsar produced a letter offering us diplomatic and trading agreements which, quite naturally, I was happy to accept on behalf of the King!"

So, finally, it was time to depart in the *Edward* for London. Our spirits were high, though our hearts were also filled with grief for the other two ships of our fleet of whom no more had been heard or seen since that terrible storm. It was apparent all had perished. In fact, both missing ships were found later that spring by Russian fishermen. May God have mercy on their souls.

We received a mixed reception on our return. On the surface, it seemed the voyage had failed. No northeast passage to the riches of the Orient had been found. Nevertheless, my seamanship had not only yielded us a safe return, but changed trading and politics for ever. It had paved the way for Sebastian Cabot to receive a Royal Charter establishing the Muscovy Company. It could now take advantage of the new trading opportunities available to the English in Russia and the continued dream of similar opportunities in China, if a north-east sea passage could ever be discovered in the future.

But my story isn't quite over. I want to tell you about my next voyage back there two years later. A voyage I would regard as even more significant than the first in terms of my personal legacy to the nation. The convoy consisted of just three ships: two merchant ships from theMuscovy Company – my old ship, the *Edward Bonaventura*, along with the *Philip and Mary* – and the 22-ton pinnace, the *Serchthrift*.

We departed Ratcliffe on April the 23rd 1556 and by April the 25th, we had reached the mouth of the Thames at Gravesend from where Mr. Cabot himself, now 82 years old, bid us farewell in grand style. He was in fine spirits and accompanied by all manner of gentlefolk. He handed out alms to those on the quayside and bid them pray for

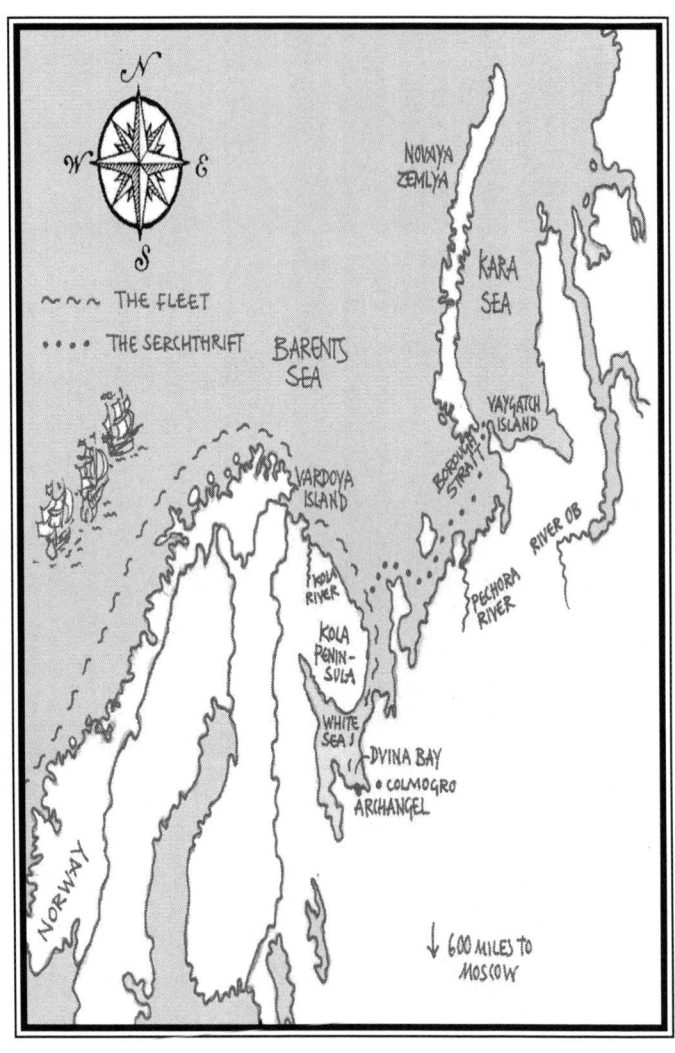

Stephen Borough's second voyage to find a north-east passage to China

the success of our voyage. There was a banquet awaiting us and music accompanied our revelry.

"Now, Mr. Borough," said he. "We couldn't let you go this time without a proper farewell. All our hopes are on you, sir, to finish what you started."

"I aim to do my very best, sir. And this is indeed a fine way to leave!"

The old man laughed. "Then let us eat and dance and toast this fine pinnace of yours to bring us success! To the *Serchthrift!*"

"The *Serchthrift!*" cried all, in unison.

At Vardoya Island, the merchant ships followed my previous route past the Kola Peninsula into the White Sea where they then proceeded to Moscow as before and continued their trading activities. But I joined the little pinnace with the intention of heading east with my crew of nine – including, for the second time, my brother William. Our goal? Yet again to search for a north-east passage to China and to explore even further east than any Western European before us. With mixed emotions and memories of the previous voyage, its losses and its triumphs, we parted from the convoy. Once again, fear and trepidation mingled with anticipation throughout the entire crew. Before heading away from the Kola Peninsula, whilst at anchor at the mouth of the River Kola, we met up with some Russian fishermen in their *lodias,* with whom we passed a little time. One in particular, Gabriel, offered us considerable help and reassurance about our proposed exploration, despite our very rudimentary understanding of each other's language. I did manage to compile a list of helpful words for, without these men, our progress would have been considerably slower and more dangerous.

For example, *cowghtie coteat* means 'what call you this', *iomme lemaupes* is 'thank you' and *avanchy thocke* means – importantly – 'get thee hence'. All most useful, to be sure. They showed us great kindness, hauling a barrel of beer some two miles and providing some mead to help ease our fear of the unknown.

We departed on June the 22nd, guided by Gabriel and other *lodias*, for the water beneath us was, at that point, barely five feet deep, until we reached a small island where we tarried awhile to collect driftwood and fresh water, before proceeding eastward once again. Before long, our initial fears of the unknown were justified. At the mouth of the Pechora River, we began to encounter monstrous heaps of floating ice which, at first, I mistook for islands. It was a fearful experience and took all our strength and seamanship to avoid crashing into them.

Soon afterwards, we became aware of an overwhelming presence alongside the pinnace. Some of the crew feared a Kraken was finally upon us. However, once it drew alongside, it became clear that it was a whale! The creature was as wide as our vessel, being some 10 feet and longer than our 22 feet. It was so near that a sword could have pierced it! The crew and I were terrified. I called them together and bade them tell the creature to depart henceforth.

"Avanchy thocke!" We screamed at the top of our voices. "Be gone!"

To our surprise, it complied and dove. The noise was terrible and we were in awe of the creature, thanking God once more to have been saved from a cruel fate.

We reached the south west coast of Novaya Zemlya Island on August the 1st. We knew the name from Loshak, another of the Russian *lodia* fishermen, who had accompanied us and given us further eastward instructions in search of the entrance to the River Ob, through which, he said, a direct route to China might be followed. This was, of course, extremely encouraging for us all. We proceeded towards the Kara Sea via the strait between Novaya Zemlya and Vaygach Island. I was rowed ashore this bleak and featureless place with my brother William and I could sense a growing bemusement in the sailors. There were William and I, armed with my navigational instruments – I clutching a wooden box containing my compass, a compass of variation, a planimetrum, my demounted cross-staff, my astrolabe, parchment, inkhorn and quill pens – to record our findings. It must have appeared the most incongruous sight to those men. I looked at William and we caught one to the other a smile on our ice-laden faces. "Well, William," said I. "What do you think mother would say if she could see us now?"

"I'll be bound she would tell us to wash and shave ourselves, Stephen," he replied. "For we do not smell or look at our best to be alighting a new land!"

We all laughed and the crew's anxiety was somewhat lessened. Once ashore, the men watched for any adverse change in weather or sea conditions, any unfriendly approaches of man or beast, any dangers whatever they could perceive in this desolate, treeless environment, whilst we set to our task.

Once back on board the *Serchthrift*, I carried out my calculations and turned my observations into a new reading of latitude, surveying and creating our navigational charts. I renamed that strait after us both. Borough Straits.

After three weeks at Vaygach, I felt we were close to a breakthrough. We were almost in the Kara Sea and the wide estuary of the River Ob would be unmissable, according to Loshak. But, once again our voyage was thwarted by the inclement conditions, the harshness of which I had never seen before nor did I ever see again. Vast floes of ice, hurricane force winds, rain and fog in addition to the lack of daylight left us with no alternative but to abandon the search on August the 4th. I was heartbroken.

We returned in atrocious conditions to the relative safety of the White Sea and proceeded to Colmogro some miles up the Dvina River. We felt fortunate to have survived. After overwintering in Colmogro, we set our sails for home once the weather improved. Despite our failure to find the north-east passage to China, we were able to draw complete navigational charts from Colmogro back to Vardoya Island. These charts were to set a standard, reliable route for all future voyages of Muscovy Company merchant ships through the White Sea. Our voyage of exploration had not been entirely in vain.

And so, my attempts to locate a north-east passage to the Orient were over. My life afterwards was a fair reflection, I believe, of the regard with which I was now held. On learning that Richard Chancellor had perished on this last voyage, I was appointed Chief Pilot to the Muscovy Company – yet another honour.

I was very dissatisfied with the low professional standards of English seamanship and my experiences now told me that this had to change if England was to regain long-term trading supremacy. I obtained permission for the translation of Martin Cortes' wonderful book on navigation *Arte de Navigar* and its adoption revolutionised the expertise of English Masters, placing them ever afterwards on a level playing field with our Portuguese and Spanish rivals. Indeed, I was invited to Seville, where I was showered with honours and gifts, including a pair of scented gloves worth five or six ducats.

I frequently sailed again to Russia with the Muscovy Company, but my 'pioneering' days were over. Instead, until my death, I continued to receive the most honourable appointments. In 1574, I was appointed adviser to Martin Frobisher's expeditions to find a north-west passage to the Orient and, finally, I was elected Master of Trinity House.

I ended my days at my house 'Goodsight' in Chatham with my second wife, Joanna, whom I had married in 1563 following Eleanora's death two years earlier. Joanna and I produced five further children. Following my death in 1584, I was buried with full naval honours at St. Mary's Church, Chatham, where a memorial plaque can still be found.

And what of my little brother, William? He continued in the Muscovy Company and was pivotal in protecting the new Baltic Sea ports and Russian trade routes from acts of piracy. His reputation led Sir Francis Drake to engage him as second in command in his strikes against the Spanish in 1587, in the lead up to the Spanish Armada. There was no great rapport between the two, but Drake recognised William's prowess as a fighting Master. During the raid which took place on April the 12th 1587, their differences – audacity against caution – led to Sir Francis putting William in irons for cowardice and shipped back to England.

William pleaded his case to Queen Elizabeth, whose sweet disposition at Sir Francis Drake's successes, led her to dismiss the case, have my brother released and promoted to Controller of the Navy on the Thames, far away from Sir Francis Drake's home port of Plymouth. William also turned his attention, like me, to the training and seamanship skills of naval officers. He published several books, found himself a wife who was the granddaughter of a former Lord Mayor of London and sailed against the Spanish Armada in 1588.

My dear brother died fifteen years after me in 1599.

The Muscovy Company never did find a north-east passage to the Orient though my son, Christopher, who became an agent for the Company, played a pivotal role in making six expeditions from the Russian White Sea through to the tropical Caspian Sea, the Iranian terminus from China and the Orient.

Towards the end of my life, I felt a profound sense of peace, giving little thought to how I might be regarded back in Northam. Yet, more than four hundred years later, I cannot help but feel a lasting sense of sorrow that I am barely remembered in the place I was born and raised. But there it is. My story is done and it's time for me to stop.

I would like to know one thing, though. What do *you* think? Should the Borough family have more than a housing estate and a road to commemorate our achievements?

Chapter 3

The Lord of the Manor
16th April 1586

The thick, wooden door of Place House opens with a clunk and a creak. One by one, a family steps out, all dressed in their finest clothes. A woman, clearly in charge of organising the procession, gathers teenage children to her sides, ushers the servants to stand behind them and finally peers into the darkness within. Shortly afterwards, an elegant gentleman appears. He is dressed fashionably in his doublet – a stiff, boned coat covered in black velvet – and short, loose trousers, finely embroidered, rust-coloured and commonly known as hose. He steps outside and breathes in the air. Smiling fondly at his family, he closes the door, embraces his wife and children, then sets off purposefully along Allhalland Street, followed by an assorted collection of family and household staff.

Sir Richard Grenville, Lord of the Manor of Bideford, has chosen to live here with his family. Even though he has bigger and more comfortable houses on the north coast of Cornwall, he loves this town. *His* town. The town where he was born. He loves the proud looks of his wife,

Sir Richard and his family in Conduit Lane

Mary, daughter Ursula and sons John and Bernard and the way the heads of everyone he encounters turn to pay their respects.

Women curtsey. Men touch their hats as he passes wishing him a simple "Good mornin', sir." Braver ones shout "God bless 'ee, sir. Safe passage!" Sir Richard acknowledges their greetings with a wave of his hand. As the procession turns right down Conduit Lane, the narrow alley leading to the Quay, everyone walks in single file. Sir Richard places his feet with considerable care to avoid the filth and sewage that runs freely down there from splashing onto his stockinged legs and polished shoes. He glances behind and motions to the women to lift their skirts above their ankles.

Once he reaches the Quay, Sir Richard passes the time of day with men sitting outside one of the taverns, smoking rough Spanish baccy in long, white clay pipes. He sniffs the air, thick with the aroma of tobacco, mingled with a warm, ale-fuelled fug coming from inside the tavern. Ah, how he wishes he had time to pass there today. But he must get on. The smells of freshly-tarred timbers, ropes and the salty stench of the Torridge drift towards Sir Richard on a stiff south-easterly breeze, bringing him back to the task at hand. Such familiarity tugs at his heart – his hopes for a good spring voyage, his yearning to remain here with his family, his anticipation of glory for Queen Elizabeth.

He makes his way down towards the bridge where a ship's boat is waiting with three uniformed oarsmen at the ready. Sir Richard turns to Lady Mary and his children. He embraces each of them once more, climbs down the wooden ladder attached to the Quay wall and steps with ease into the small rowing boat. He waves to the watching crowd who have gathered on the Quay and spilled onto the Bridge to cheer him on his way as the oars are lowered and the little boat is pushed away from the wall.

A few minutes later, the boat is alongside a beautiful galleon, moored in the middle of the Torridge. Sir Richard, an agile military man, hoists himself onto it, helped by waiting crew. The galleon is of Spanish origin and Sir Richard gazes around him proudly. He recalls the day he captured her on the high seas for Queen Elizabeth only a year earlier. What a battle! What a fine vessel! He has had her beautifully refitted here in Bideford. Her old Spanish name, *Santa Maria*, has been replaced now with a fine new piece of oak on which is carved the new name he has chosen, *Galleon Dudley*, in honour of the Earl of Leicester. Also waiting for him in the fleet are his beloved ships *Tiger* and *Roebuck*. Now he, the *Galleon Dudley*'s Commander, stands proudly on her quarter-deck, surveying the activity on the ship in front of him. He watches the carpenters, sail-makers and deckhands, all fully engaged on their last-minute tasks. He walks down to the fo'c'sle, acknowledging the respect of the crew on both port and starboard. Beyond the bowsprit, he can feel the river Torridge beckoning him down the estuary towards the Atlantic. He looks at the sky. It is cloudy, heavy. And the tide? Almost full. Another few minutes and all will be ready.

He packs his pipe with baccy and stands, erect, reflecting undisturbed for a time whilst all goes on behind him. Then he turns and makes his way to the Captain's cabin where he installs himself at his desk, opens his personal Journal and takes up his quill.

Sir Richard Grenville aboard the Galleon Dudley

"Today, this 16th day of April 1586, I am beginning this, my second voyage across the Atlantic to Roanoke Island in Virginia. Should disaster befall me, I pray this document will survive and my brief account of what has taken place thus far will live on. I want it to be known that, despite what may be said, my allegiance remains, at all times, to Her Majesty Queen Elizabeth of England.

For me, this most essential part of my life began less than twelve months ago. July the 11th 1585. What a day that was! After three months at sea where we were fully occupied with enemy engagements, unforeseen dangers and near tragedies, I, Sir Richard Grenville, became the first Englishman to found a colonial settlement in North America! It was a kind accident of fate, in truth, that had brought Captains Amadas and Barlow to Roanoke the year previous (1584) in their preliminary exploration of the coast thereabouts. It was they who had reported back to my cousin Raleigh and the English Court on its suitability to the founding of the first English colony and it was they who had brought back two natives, one of whom – Manteo – became critical in our dealings with the local tribes prior to the construction of the fort.

Upon arrival in Roanoke, those in charge alongside me: Ralph Lane, John White, fleet commander Simon Ferdinando (I do not trust him) and I were also in agreement that Roanoke was an ideal location to commence the building of our fort, relatively easy to protect because of the visibility, being almost surrounded by the mainland. We set to, familiarising ourselves with the territory and, barely a week later, the time was right to begin our mission on the mainland in earnest. Some of my men rowed me across, whereupon I claimed the entire area for my beloved Queen. Already named Virginia in her honour the year before by Raleigh, yet waiting for that claim to be acted upon, it was I, Richard Grenville, who was the first man to begin the task. Yes, July the 11th. How proud I felt on that day!

It was at this point that the aforementioned native, Manteo, became useful, as we were able to make good contacts with three tribes of natives over the next three weeks or so. They were surprisingly friendly at first. We exchanged gifts, shared food and wine with them. Indeed, they seemed quite happy for us to build a fort and a settlement on Roanoke. We began work without delay and, on August the 5th, I was able to despatch John Arundel back to the Queen's court with news.

But I had a suspicion that problems were already beginning. Arguments and bad feeling between some of us and the natives was growing. Co-operation was subsequently withdrawn by the natives, following an earlier incident involving the theft of a silver cup. Now I admit I am not a patient man and I showed little sympathy or mercy. The stealing of the silver cup was, I believed, the right time for me to show them that they now had new masters and that kind of behaviour would not be tolerated. Yes, I destroyed their crops, upon which they relied for food. I had to establish a new order.

Despite our differences, by August the 25th, I considered things were sufficiently well organised to leave Ralph Lane as Commander of Roanoke Fort and sail back to England for more supplies to help sustain my fledgling colony. I was duty bound to return to England before the winter weather set in if I was to make this return voyage with all they would need. That was my plan. Yes. A good plan. And now we must find out if that plan has worked. For today, the return voyage begins. And of it, I will report at a later date. God speed to all who sail with me this day. God bless my wife and family. God save the Queen."

Sir Richard lays down his pen and returns once more to the quarter-deck. He is proud of the work his Bideford shipwrights have carried out on the galleon, turning her into one his dear Queen could be proud to call her own. Then he thinks once more about the 108 souls he took to Roanoke the previous year and whom he will soon see again, God willing. Men so close to his heart. Men who had also built and fitted out the ships for that first voyage here in Bideford. Bideford men he had hand-picked; experienced mariners he had taken with him into those uncharted waters – men he holds in the highest regard for their skill and bravery. Men no longer here in Bideford but hopefully waiting to greet him once more on Roanoke.

But Sir Richard is worried. If the colony's a success, it will bring great rewards for him in the court of Queen Elizabeth and huge trading opportunities to his beloved home port of Bideford. But what if it has not survived the winter? He knows he must face the possibility that it might be so. Sir Richard knocks the ash from his pipe into the Torridge and takes a deep breath. Soon he will know. Soon they'll have new supplies and goods with which to bargain. Soon he'll know if the town's good folk have been justly rewarded for all their hard work and loyalty to him. After all, those qualities ensured he got to Roanoke in the first place. But there's still a lot to do. He goes down to the main deck and looks over the port side at the water level. The tide is full now. A final wave to his family and townsfolk. It's time to get under way!

The Lord Of The Manor

The end of the story …

Sadly, when Sir Richard arrived two and a half months later on July the 3rd 1586, the fort – along with all those he had left behind – had completely disappeared. There was no way that Sir Richard could have known that they had left Roanoke only one week before he arrived and returned to England with Sir Francis Drake, who had also paid a visit there with supplies. They would have crossed somewhere in the Atlantic.

Sir Francis had found many of the settlers sick, wounded and weak, begging to return to England. It would not have been easy for them. They would certainly have found the climate harsher than what they were used to and dangerous in many ways. Unknown plants and wildlife would have proved a challenge. They were trying to settle in a land that was already home to North American Indians, who were increasingly unhappy that they were there. The settlers would also have come across diseases and illnesses they had never encountered before. Food and water may have run out. Perhaps their newly-planted crops had not grown …

Sir Richard's colony had failed. So did the next attempt made by John White in 1587. In fact, no-one knows for certain what happened to those settlers – who became known as The Lost Colony – but research shows it is likely that they left the island for another, Hatteras, and that they continued to live their lives as part of the native population. Other attempts eventually did succeed and Jamestown, Virginia was successfully settled in the early 1600s. Subsequently, Bideford was able to take advantage of Sir Richard's achievements when the town finally began to trade with the new colonies. Soon Bideford would import more tobacco than any other port in the country except London.

It can be difficult to grasp the significance of Sir Richard Grenville's achievement. One way to think of it is to liken Sir Richard and his men to astronauts and that first voyage to man's first moon landing in 1969. The perils of exploring uncharted parts of our own planet would have been similar back then to those of that lunar landing. When Sir Richard first felt the earth of Roanoke Island under his feet, he had no idea what or whom he might find there. The fine seamen of Bideford, Sir Richard Grenville's 'oceanautes', may have taken small steps by today's standards, but they were giant leaps by men of the Old World into this unknown New World. Giant leaps that would forge Bideford's fame and fortune for the next 200 years.

Ready to sail – the Galleon Dudley, the Tiger and the Roebuck

Chapter 4
The Most Unusual Stranger
1585–1587

Let's step back for a moment to the autumn before the last story. It's late October 1585 and Sir Richard is sailing home to Bideford. The townsfolk know through word of mouth that he's finally coming back after more than six months with the little fleet he took on his voyage. They also know by word of mouth that he will be bringing back another ship, one he has captured along the way. They don't know exactly what he's been up to or what he's done. They don't know that he is returning from his first voyage to Roanoke Island in North America. Nor do they know or understand that he has founded the first English colony there. He is always up to something. But an extraordinary thing is about to happen in Bideford, something as unique as the founding of the colony itself, something that will be quite unimaginable to any of them until they have seen it for themselves. This time, there is someone with Sir Richard who is very special indeed …

In Place House, at the west end of the Bridge, Sir Richard's family received news over a week ago that he was safely back in England. They knew that he had captured a Spanish galleon for the Queen, sailed back across the Atlantic in her to Plymouth where he received a rousing welcome when he dropped anchor outside the walled town of Sutton. Yesterday, Lady Mary was informed that her husband was sailing back up to Bideford in the galleon, bringing his other ships with him to refit. Messages of sightings had arrived from Clovelly and, most recently, news from Appledore that the fleet had crossed the Bar and would be arriving on the Quay this very afternoon! Lady Mary has ordered the preparation of a great banquet for her husband and there is all manner of hustle and bustle in the kitchens and dining hall.

On the Quay, word is spreading that Sir Richard's return is imminent. The people know now that he will be on the Spanish ship they have heard about. Crowds are beginning to gather there and spreading on to the bridge, watching for the appearance of masts down river.

"Aye! Aye! 'Ere 'ee comes! I can see 'un!" says Thomas Andrews, leaning over the Quay edge at an alarming angle, no doubt fuelled by ale he has been drinking in the King's Arms. "Tidn't the Tiger in front, though. 'Tis that there Spanish galleon, you!" His rich booming voice is aimed at anyone who wants to listen. Now he turns to the crowd behind him. "Sir Richard be on the galleon!"

Murmurs grow louder and anticipation mounts. Necks crane like swans downriver towards Cleave. Little children run through skirts, stockings and boots to get to the front of the Quay, squealing with excitement. Now, some can see sails being dropped and drawn in like washing on a windy day as the ships approach, sitting high and proud on the full tide, distant but audible instructions on board getting ever closer. Cheers are starting to ring round, getting louder, nudging and nods exchanged among the fuss on the narrow Quay. At last, the Saint George's Cross ensign is clearly visible on the main mast of the galleon and a roar goes up.

"'Tis true, then! He's back!" Thomas shouts his news to friends still in the tavern. "And on the Spanish ship, too! Come out 'yer and see fur yourselves!"

More men drift out of the tavern to watch the ships drop anchor, knocking the ash out of their long white pipes on the tavern walls. They can see Sir Richard standing proud on the quarterdeck of the galleon as it swings round at the top of the tide and the ships are secured. Those who can read, strain their eyes to see the unfamiliar words of her name: Santa Maria.

"Welcome 'ome, Sir Richard!" Thomas Andrews sets up a cheer, repeated by many in the crowd, as they throw their hats in the air, clapping and hooraying with joy. The noise echoes across the river and back again from East of the Water, when the Lord of the Manor is lowered in a cradle over the side of the galleon into a gig that will take him to shore. But then, all of a sudden, the cheers fade and die, replaced by gasps of horror. Hands cover mouths in fear and a disbelieving hush spreads across the crowd. Thomas and his friends stand there, open-mouthed.

"Whathevver ... ?" Thomas begins to speak, but cannot find the words to finish his sentence.

Someone is with Sir Richard. Someone very strange. Someone the likes of whom none in Bideford has ever seen before. A strange young man but curiously dressed, curious entirely in appearance, is following Sir Richard off the ship, using one of the cannons to lower himself

The Most Unusual Stranger

onto the gig. He is being beckoned there by Sir Richard himself. He is agile, thin, but has the wild stare of a scared animal. The gig is rowed by crew to the shore while the stranger is staring all around him, terrified of all he can see.

"Make way, make way there!" cries the ship's bo's'un, having climbed up onto the Quay to clear a passage for Sir Richard. He is all too aware of the gawping faces and the unusual sight of the stranger from the other side of the Atlantic.

The crowds begin to part as Sir Richard alights, climbing a wooden ladder on to the Quay. The stranger cowers in the gig, as frightened to encounter the crowd as they are to encounter him. Once more, Sir Richard beckons the stranger to follow him, which he does obediently. His eyes dart back and forth at the crowd, his arms sometimes raised as if to protect himself from attack when the murmurs swell. But there is a proud demeanour about him also.

The townsfolk have seen a few strangers in Bideford before, 'furriners' they call them, dark-skinned ones brought back from Africa, but they've never seen one like this before. Usually, furriners are finely dressed by the ship's Captain in the clothes of an Englishman, shown off and displayed like living treasure. But this one is different. He looks like a man and yet … not like a man they have ever seen before. He wears no clothes to speak of, but has a woollen blanket wrapped around him, which one of the crew was ordered to give him to protect against the chilly October wind. Even his feet are bare and there are strange ink patterns all over his skin. His hair is braided with unfamiliar bird feathers. He has necklaces made of beads, shells and what look like the teeth of cats.

By this time, Thomas Andrews is clutching his hat with both hands, reduced to silence as Sir Richard ushers the stranger along towards the Bridge where they turn right towards Place House. "Why idn't he dressed up fine like the others?" he says. "'Tis a bit frightening for these yur kiddies t'see 'un like that!" Thomas scratches his head, looking at the women standing beside him. They are whispering to each other behind their hands. But the 'kiddies' are fascinated. As the spectacle approaches, the women grab them away from their grandstand views at the front and shield their eyes as this most unusual stranger scurries along behind Sir Richard towards …

"Now then! This can't be right!" Thomas whispers to the women. "Can you see where 'ees gwain? Sir Richard is taking him straight into Place House, dressed like that! Whathevver will Lady Mary say? Whathevver is going on?"

The Most Unusual Stranger arrives on Bideford Quay

18 months later – March the 27th 1588:

The bells of St. Mary's are ringing out as clear as the fine spring Sunday morning they accompany. The Lord of the Manor and his family are in Church. A few women and children are gathering in Church Walk. They've heard there's a Grenville Christening this morning and are taking time before Sunday dinner to find out who the Lord of the Manor has brought to dedicate to God. At last, the church doors open but what they see isn't at all what they expected.

"No … 't'idn possible," says Mary Allen, arms folded around her shawl. "'Tis that there stranger, i'dn it, coming out the Church? You knaw, Charity, that there fithered one with no clothes and necklaces on that us seed last year, 'ee 'oo come 'ome with Sir Richard that there time? You remember, don't 'ee?"

Her friend, Charity Saunders, is leaning on her daughter's shoulders to get a better view of the Grenville entourage and straining her neck to see the person Mary is talking about. "You'm right, Mary. 'Tis exaccerly the same one, you," she replies.

"And jus' you look at that finery 'ee be dressed in now! Looks like 'tis 'ee who've been christened! But I'd recognise 'ees face anywhere. Those eyes!"

"Well. Fancy that," exclaims Charity. "A furrin' Christian, right yer in Bideford. Us nivver had one o'they before, did us?"

As the family begins its procession from St. Mary's back towards Place House, Mary lowers her voice. "I do think Sir Richard hev done this deliberate, you knaw. So us can zee 'ow this yur boy 'ave altered by not bein' a heathen no more!"

The Most Unusual Stranger

The two women stand on tiptoe and shade their eyes against the mid-morning sun to get a better look. The entourage is led by Sir Richard and Lady Mary. The stranger follows on behind them and then the rest of the family, gradually making their way out of the church.

Mary and Charity are seamstresses with fine eyes for detail and quality on the clothes of the wealthy. As the stranger passes, they look at each other as they recognise the linen shirt, the ruff as well as the royal blue doublet which has long sleeves and wrist ruffs. The stranger's hose and shoes also look familiar.

"Did'n us see young Master John Grenville wearing this yer stuff a year or two back, when 'ee used to come to Church with 'ees father?" whispers Charity.

"You'm right, maid," says Mary quietly. "Us sayed at the time 'ow fine 'twas, did'n us? And look at 'ees hair! No more braids and fithers now."

"No! 'Tis washed, cut an' coiffed like a gentleman." exclaims Charity. No mistakin', though. 'Tis that furriner, a'right."

No wonder Mary and Charity are confused. Over the last 18 months, the stranger has become a loyal and faithful servant to the Grenville family. He is speaking broken English now, every bit as good as some of the locals. And this very morning, the stranger brought home from North America by Sir Richard was baptised a Christian and given the name Raleigh. Never before in England has such an occasion taken place. There could not be a clearer demonstration of Sir Richard's intention. Raleigh has been brought to Bideford and today transformed into a Christian manservant. Word would surely spread. He may not be the first North American Indian brought back

Raleigh with the Grenvilles after his Christening

to England, but never before has such a privilege been bestowed upon a servant from that continent.

Less than 12 months later, Sir Richard will be fighting the Spanish Armada, never making another planned return to Roanoke.

As for Raleigh? Raleigh will die on April the 7th 1589, the victim of a fever that will also claim the life of Sir Richard's daughter, Rebecca, and another of his servants. Raleigh will be given a Christian burial and his body will be buried in St Mary's churchyard. A headstone will be paid for by Sir Richard to forever mark the spot where the only American Indian to be baptised and buried as a Christian in England, is laid to rest in Bideford.

If you visit St. Mary's churchyard now, you can find a record of Raleigh's Christening and his death in the Parish Registers. You can see that the spelling on each is different. We must assume that the Baptism name 'Raleigh' is the one given him by Sir Richard Grenville himself, perhaps after his cousin Sir Walter Raleigh. But you will not find the original headstone that was paid for by the Lord of the Manor. The significance of this piece of history wasn't realised and Raleigh's headstone – some say on the east and some say on the west side of the church – was never looked after. It disappeared over time when repair and rebuilding works were carried out on the church during the 19th and 20th centuries.

However, you can find a memorial plaque in St Mary's Church. When the story was once again given publicity in 2008, action was taken to reinstate a memorial to Raleigh and, in 2012, a group of American visitors from Manteo, now twinned with Bideford, was present for the ceremony that ensured that the memory or Raleigh and his unique place in Bideford history would never again be forgotten.

Chapter 5
The Hero of the Pestilence 1646

OYEZ! OYEZ! OYEZ!
Ye townspeople of Bideford, 'tis with much sorrow that this proclamation is made to announce the passing of Mr. John Strange, merchant, ship owner and Mayor of this town, who succumbed to the Pestilence early this 19th day of July, the year of our Lord 1646. Mayor Strange did become Mayor for the fourth time when the Mayor previous did flee the town following the onset of the Pestilence that has shown us some of our darkest days and taken so many of our kith and kin. Mayor Strange did voluntarily retake the office, comforted and helped this town's residents as they suffered from the Sore Fever, but with not a care for his own wellbeing. Mayor Strange thought nothing of entering the houses of those who were

grievous ill. He arranged burial of the dead and offered succour to families left destitute through the passing of their loved ones. Without Mayor Strange, this Pestilence might have spread outward to the countryside beyond. Only by his orders to safeguard the entrances to the town has this not happened. Though the devil's disease renders us weary and depleted, the efforts of Mayor Strange leave our town proud, surviving and eternally grateful to him.

May God have mercy on the soul of John Strange and may he rest in peace.

Interment will take place on the 20th day of July, in St Mary's Church at 10 o'clock.

GOD SAVE THE KING!

The Town Crier announces the death of John Strange

The Hero Of The Pestilence

Well, that's over. I do believe it was the most difficult proclamation I have ever had to make. Better get it posted on the door of the King's Arms for them all to see. Now ... where's my Martha? Oh no ... the blacksmith is heading toward me. I have no desire to speak to anyone today. I need to get away from here.

"Ah, 'tis a sad day, Mr. Phillips. You must feel it more than most of us here, I reckon."

I return the blacksmith's handshake with as much grace as I can manage. "Thank you, James. There's no denying it." It's about all I can say, my throat being choked up with sorrow. More and more people are starting to crowd in on me.

"Yes, thank you James. It has been a hard day for us both."

Ah, there she is at last! Thank the Lord! Martha briskly picks up the bell she had rung before I began the proclamation. "Come along, Richard." She guides me away from the well-meaning crowd towards the tavern door.

I take the little hammer from the pocket of my robe and hold out my hand. Martha knows the routine. She delves into the deep recesses of her dress and produces four nails from the supply we keep especially for posting the proclamations. People are shuffling, shuffling, ever nearer and nearer. All I want to do is finish the task and get home. Finally it's done.

Gently, Martha takes my arm and we begin our little walk back to Tower Street. Ah, my Martha. My dearest wife. She knows what a struggle today has been for me and now she is protecting me from all the muttering men and women, all wanting to share their own memories and stories of John Strange.

As we head up Conduit Lane and turn left into Allhalland Street. I catch her watching me from the corner of my eye. I know she can see the pain and sadness etched on this old face of mine for I have seen it myself in father's mirror glass.

"Good crowd today, dear," she says. There she goes, trying to break through my silence.

"Yes," I reply. "'Twas only right. How could our family have survived without him?" The ache in my throat is spreading and my voice is beginning to tremble as we turn into Church Walk.

"I know. All the help he give us with little Jacob. And with father. And we never had the chance to say thank you properly before … well, before he passed."

I know that quiet tone in her voice. She is weeping softly, although she turns her face away so that I cannot see it. She is so brave. But, after a few more steps, she can no longer restrain herself.

"And it isn't over yet! Why, us buried eighteen last month and forty-odd more in St Mary's this month with one third of it still to go! And that's just the ones us knows about. Oh dear, if only Mister Strange had still been Mayor before that Spanish vessel come in to the Quay. He already knew the Sore Fever was in Spain. He knew about they black rats and they fleas. He would've stopped the ship from unloading its wool and spreading them all about. Not like that other one who let it all in."

"'Tis no good supposin' now, Martha. What's done is done. Us could also say IF they three Ravening boys hadn't played on they woolsacks which turned out to be full of they fleas carrying the disease in the first place. And IF young Tommy Caldwell hadn't left they others behind to come and play with Jacob, then perhaps he and father would still be with us now."

In trying to stop her going down this foolish road of 'what if's', I hear myself reinforcing it. But there. It all needs to be out and said, I suppose. We both need to lance this boil of grief we carry. We are half way up Church Walk now and, just for a moment, I feel the urge to lean on the Church wall and look at the graves of our son and my father. It's no good. I can no longer hold myself apart from the sorrow. It is overwhelming. I feel a waterfall of tears spill from my eyes onto my robes. They look like blood.

"There, there, Richard, 'tis like you said. There's nothing that can be done to change anything now. We must just be grateful that Mister Strange had the courage to take control again when he did. It took a brave man to step into the breach like that."

"'Twas when he put they sentries on the entrances to the town and stopped people leaving and comin' in, that was surely a blessing for everyone."

Thinking about what the Mayor had done to help us was now helping me. I had to continue, to have courage for his sake and that of my own family. "Now we must stay strong for the other little ones. 'Tis fortunate that Mister Strange and the father of they Ravening boys …"

"The doctor, you mean?"

"Yes, the doctor. 'Twas he that showed us how important it is to keep clean. Us nivver knew half of that cleanliness business afore, did us? Nor how to handle the dead properly, getting them collected and buried quick. 'Tis our good fortune that Dr Ravening is still with us. It must be so hard for he, losing all three of his boys to it and still to minister to the rest of us."

The Town Crier and his wife in Church Walk

"Yes, you'm right, Richard. We must be grateful, true enough." She squeezes my shoulders.

"Well, 'tis approaching dinner time. I expect mother's waiting on us with the maidens. May God keep us safe and may God bless the soul of Mister Strange. This town will never forget him. And that's the truth."

As Richard and Martha Phillips join their arms together and continue their heavy-hearted walk home, they are unaware that the Black Death will continue for another seven months and take, in total, 229 Bideford souls, including Mr. Phillips himself, his mother and one of their daughters.

In due course, a memorial to John Strange will be erected in St Mary's Church by the Captain of a ship who was rescued by him after being shipwrecked nearby. It was only when the Captain returned to Bideford some time after the plague had subsided, that he learned that the man who had saved his life had died. The memorial can still be found in St. Mary's Church.

Chapter 6

The First English Dustman 1673

The Dialect of Davey Heard, the Town Scavenger

"Well, 'twas like this yer. They come up with this notion and now ev'ryone is starting to call me the Dustman instead of the Town Scavenger, which has been my work now since father died and I took it over from 'ee. Perhaps I'm not the first Dustman in the land, an' Lord knaws why 'tis called dust, for 'tis anything but. However, I shall call myself the first Dustman because who else do'ee knaw who 'as all these yer baccy 'ogsheads lyin' around? Let me tell 'ee how it come about.

Well, they'm a filthy lot in Bideford and that's the truth. I've been telling they municipals for years that us should be doin' summin' 'bout these yer stinking dunghills and other filth in the town. If I'd 'ad my way, I'd have taken some of 'em to the Quarter Sessions for the mess they makes. Their hogs an' swine runs amuk through the town and on the Quay in the summer, well the stink! 'Tis just

Sanitary conditions in Nunnery Walk

shocking, you! And throwing all that stuff straight out the winders onto the street and into the 'edges. 'T'ain't right, you. 'T'ain't right for they little nippers to have all that filth around. No wonders they'm badly all the time and dyin' too, some of 'em. In a minute, us'll have the Sore Fever back yer again an' no Mayor Strange to 'elp us this time. And they old'uns, they'm the worst. Don't know no better, I'm thinking. I've always done the best I can to keep things in order but 'tis nigh on impossible, there's so much of it, you see.

Well, blow me down if they 'aven't listened to I – Davey Heard, the Town Scavenger! I was talking to the Crier t'other day and 'ee said to me that at the Borough Quarter Sessions on the twelfth of May, th'Earl of Bath was telled off good an' proper for allowing a pool of filth to stay in the same place, because it was dangerous for the King's lieges who wuz passing! Well, I'm not so sure why the King's men should be traited special like but, anyway, not only that, Crier told me that Thomas Lake, 'ee up Bull Hill, 'ee was telled the same thing for allowing filth and dung to lie against 'ees garden wall! An' old widder Bragg, 'er in Nunnery, 'er got a good tellin' off for havin' a filthy heap of dung in 'er bed-chamber if you hevver did!

Well, all this yer got me to wonderin, how'm they gwain' to keep control of it? For 'tis only four instances in one Quarter! But yesterday the Crier told me more! The Justices 'ave got the bull by the 'orns now and issued a 'edict' (I think 'tis a fancy word for some new rules) and 'tis signed by Mayor John Davie. Crier's off out now to nail 'em up so's evryone in the town can see 'em and bide by 'em too. Knowing as I gits around town a fair bit as Town

Tobacco hogsheads outside King Street warehouses

Scavenger (that's how's I know so much about filth, you see), he've gived me some copies to nail up Coldharbour and thereabouts for 'tis a bit of a heave for 'un up there with all they robes of 'is. 'Ee explained to me what the seven things is and I 'as to tell all they up there too 'cos like me, they can't read proper. I can recognise most o'the words, though.

Anyways, I thought 'ee might like to hear what us be gwain' to do and how clever 'twill be using all they 'ogsheads from Virginny. Mind you, 'tis goin' to mean a lot more work for I and I shall 'ave to 'ave more 'elp, I reckon.

So, yur's the things. He've writ 'em simple and bin through 'em all with I so as I can recite 'em like 'ee. I shall have a practise to 'ee now. 'Twill be more or less like 'ee says it, I hope.

Number One. *"All dung, sweepings of the street, coal, other rubbish, loose stones or other filth is to be removed within seven days. Anyone disobeying this and seen to be disobeying by one witness on oath, willbe prosecuted."* An' quite right, too, says I!

Number Two. *"The free-running of hogs, pigs or swine through the town is forbidden."* Also 'tis only right.

Number Three. *"From this day forth, discarded tobacco hogsheads are to be used by inhabitants to dispose of rubbish. These will be provided and procured by three or four or more residents as they may consent and agree amongst themselves."* Huh! Consent and agree … that'll be interestin'.

Number Four. *"The hogsheads will be repaired and amended at the charge of the inhabitants of this town."* They won't like that one little bit!

Number Five. *"The hogshead dustbins are for the use of those town residents who are unable to dispose of their rubbish*

The First English Dustman

in any other area of their properties and are to be placed in locations least offensive and decided upon by Mr. Mayor of this town." Mayor Davie 'ave already decided where they'm to be put – there's gwain' to be 30 of 'em ivrywhere from East the Bridge northwards to Maiden Street.

Number Six. *"Once the hogsheads are full, the Scavenger of the Town, or some in his behalf will be ordered to remove and empty the hogsheads away from the streets in which they are situated and into an agreed location that will cause no harm to residents."* Well, they'm goin' to 'ave to find me a site and a big ole cart fur the carryin' of they!

Number Seven. *"Detritus brought into streets for removal must be placed into hogsheads or other suitable removal receptacles within three days."* I'll let 'ee see the list of where they'm to be put. You'll be surprised and 'ow many there is!

There! I'll be bound you nivver thought I could recite all that, did 'ee? At the end, Mayor Davie says anyone 'oo disobeys these yur new rules or damages the 'ogsheads can be reported and thrown into jail until they can behave theirselves! Looks like they'm serious, don't it? I'll let 'ee knaw how us gets on but now I'm off up Coldharbour, so I'll wish 'ee all good day.

Oh! I almost forgot. Yer's the list."

High Street	3
Near the Stocks	1
New Street	2
Gunstone Lane	1
Dick Lane	1
Mill Street	3
New Kay	1
Old Kay	3

Conduit Lane	1
Near the Pit door	1
Allhalland Street	2
Bridge Street	2
Coldharbour	2
Maiden Street	2
Silver Street	1
East the Bridge Southwards	2
East the Bridge Northwards	2

The Town Scavenger posts the edicts

Chapter 7

The Potter's Son
1681

I often come out here on a Saturday afternoon. It's a beautiful walk down from my home at the top of town along the riverbank beyond the hurly-burly of the Quay. And, after the mayhem of the little school most days, I am more than ready for some peace and quiet at the end of the week. On summer days like this, I bring some bread and a piece of mother's cheese along with a small flagon of cider. I like to watch the ships come in on the full tide. On this fine June day, I have found a patch of sweet grass to sit on. It leads to a little gravel beach but the water's right in today, lapping almost at my feet. Beautiful. There are mooring posts here for rowing boats, too. From here, I can see the big merchant ships anchored further up river, nearer the bridge. There are so many of them! Most have returned from Virginia with big cargoes of tobacco, but there are others from the Mediterranean unloading wine, brandy and dried fruits and reloading with salt cod to take back there.

As I strolled along the Quay on my way here, there

were goings-on everywhere! People, hogsheads of tobacco, carts and truckles loading and unloading. Tobacco's getting big business in Bideford and people are saying it's already making the town prosperous, not only because of the plant itself, but because of the extra trade it is generating to supply goods the new colonies in America with all they need.

The river is bustling with boats of all kinds. Lighters and barges are transporting brand new parcels of earthenware goods from Potter's Pill to the ships for their return voyages to the colonies. You can see the goods all neatly packed in straw and loaded into wicker baskets. Even more barges are bringing in clay from Fremington and tempering gravel from the river's edge to keep town's potters supplied on both sides of the Torridge. There is a haze of stinking smoke everywhere from the slaughter houses and all the kilns at East the Water, Potter's Lane, Mill Street and Willett Street. Why, sometimes, it almost blocks out the sun in the late afternoon. Work never seems to stop! I have lived here all my life and I have never seen it like this!

It is more peaceful out here. I can see a boy fishing from a little rowing boat. Wait a minute … yes, it's young Philip Beale, the potter's son! Look at him. Dear little boy he is. Bright, too. A great thinker. He's been in my school several years now and, sadly, this is his last before joining his father in the pottery. It is a shame he cannot carry on to the Grammar School in Allhalland Street. But there it is. His father needs him. The boy always calls himself by his full name when anyone asks. "Philip Thomas Beale." He says it as if it was one word and it always makes me smile. Sometimes, if I require him to pay attention, I will

Mr. Drew watches Philip Beale fishing in the Torridge

also call him 'PhilipThomasBeale', as if it is one word. It makes all the children laugh, including Philip. I must make sure I teach him all I can while he's still with me. When he leaves, his only teacher will be his father and Philip's hands will not be occupied with letters and figures but with clay, firings, patterns and glazes.

Already he's looking at the afternoon sun, thinking about the time and that he should be getting back home to Potter's Lane. It looks like he has a basket full of fish in there. Enough to feed his family and some to keep for salting too. It will save Mrs. Beale some time I expect during these next busy days, until the latest commissions from the colonies are completed. Philip told me only yesterday that his father is busier than ever before. Like his own father before him, Thomas Beale has always made earthenware goods for Ireland and Wales, but Philip says he is twice as busy as before and that, in some ways, it's a good job they will no longer let his father be Mayor, because he has so much work to do. He said he has hardly seen his father for the past week, except when he goes to collect his pots between the firings.

"He looks that tired, Mr. Drew, sir, and 'tis so hot everywhere at the moment, I'm proper afraid for him sometimes that he will expire! All these things for Mr. Davie. 'Tis the biggest order he's ever had – plates, bowls, pans, candlesticks, jugs, bottle stops, platters, ovens, firebacks, chamber pots – it nivver ends! They colonials need everything!"

"Your father is working hard because he *wants* to be busy, Philip! He wants to feel useful. Things are difficult, I know, but you must try not to worry. He is a strong man."

But I had a hard time reassuring him. I have been aware for some time that Philip is troubled. Just the other morning, as I was walking the woods towards school, I found him in tears down by an old beech tree that fell in last winter's big storm.

"Now then, Philip, what's all this?" said I.

"It just isn't right, Mr. Drew."

"What isn't right, boy?"

"It's just not right that father can't be Mayor any more. The other children say it's because of the way we worship God. They call us Non-Conformists because we worship with a different preacher in the Meeting House. And it's only a secret where that is because we would get bothered if they knew where we were." All his concerns were tumbling out of him in a rush. "Course it means we don't worship in St. Mary's now but it's to the same God, isn't it, so what do it matter? Why do us have to meet in secret? And why do it mean father can't be Mayor? I don't understand, Mr. Drew!"

Philip's tears were falling free onto his shirt and his nose was running. I sat down next to him on the old tree.

"Now, look, Philip. When your Granfer came here from France it was because people there didn't like the way he worshipped God so they drove him and the others out. They called them Huguenots. The French didn't understand there *could* be a different way to worship God other than theirs. It frightened them and they started to make life very hard for Granfer. So he came here. But now it's starting again here in Bideford. It's also the reason your father's not Mayor any more. It's a shame a man as good as him isn't respected for who he is but there it is."

The boy had stopped crying. "Thank you for explaining Mr. Drew." He passed the back of his hands across his eyes and wiped them on his breeches. "I haven't been

Mr. Drew comforts Philip Beale

able to ask father or mother about it but I think I understand now." He looked up at me. His eyes were swollen and red from so many tears. "Do you think it will ever change, sir?"

"I don't know, my boy." I had dreaded the question. "I like to think so. If there is any justice, things will change."

"Do you know what I do when I feel sad and angry, Mr. Drew?"

I shook my head.

"I come fishing on the Torridge. Where it's quiet. Just me, the lapping of the water and the sound of the gulls. Out there, none of they people matter."

And so, here he is, doing what he loves to do when he's sad and angry. And I remember our conversation and feel for him and wish it were already different. I can see he's packed up for the day and is rowing towards where I'm sitting. This must be where he keeps his boat, too.

"Afternoon, Philip," I shout towards him. "Had a good day, have you?"

He looks over his shoulder and a broad smile lights up his face. He pulls in the oars and jumps out of the boat into the water.

"Good afternoon, Mr. Drew, sir." He wades in the last few yards, pulling his boat and then hooks a rope over the mooring post. "Yes, thank 'ee. And a fine catch for mother, too." He pulls the basket out of the boat onto the grass. It is full of perch and bream. "What be you doing out here?"

"Oh, probably the same as you. To get some peace and quiet."

Philip puts the basket of fish into the shade under the trees. He covers it with a muslin cloth and sits next to me

The Potter's Son

on the grass. We have a yarn about this and that. I tell him about the activity I saw on my way here. He tells me that when he left Potter's Lane this morning, he walked along Rope Walk behind the shipyard on Potter's Pill.

"There was so much going on, sir! There were ropes being braided and stretched and coiled from one end to the other. All I could smell was hemp and pitch and oil. All I could hear was the master shipwrights yelling their orders and the sound of hammers on wood. Father says it's getting busier than ever now the merchants and the ship owners are building more vessels to keep up with all the trade!"

"Yes, Bideford is becoming a prosperous town, there's no mistaking that. You had a friend, didn't you, Philip, who went to Jamestown last year? What was his name again?"

"You mean John Yeo, sir? Yes, he and his family paid ten pounds and they all went to start a new life in Virginny. Did you know him, sir?"

"No, the Yeo boys didn't get to school, I'm afraid. Such a shame."

"I miss John … often wonder how he's getting on. Granfer Beale told me about that foreigner who came to Bideford years ago with Sir Richard Grenville. He with no clothes and wearing feathers and a cats' teeth necklace? Granfer says he was from there. I wonder if John has seen any of they?"

"You know he's buried in St. Mary's churchyard, don't you? Near the West Gate.

"He nivver is!"

"It's as true as your name is Philip Thomas Beale! You go and ask your Granfer."

The boy laughs. It's good to see him relax. "I will, sir! I shall miss school but I can't wait work with father. Then he won't be so tired." He looks at the smoky sky over Potter's Pill. "There'll be twice as much smoke and sparks in the sky then!"

"I don't doubt it, my boy." I smile as he gathers his things together and hoists the basket of fish onto his shoulder.

"Goodbye Mr. Drew, sir."

"Goodbye, Philip"

As Philip walks off with his basket towards Potter's Lane, I reflect on how much I love days like this – gentle summer days when the Bar beyond us looks kindly upon our brave sailors, merchants and ship owners like Mr. Buck and Mr. Davie. I pray that they may long continue their voyages and bring prosperity to our town. I will miss that boy. His father is a lucky man. And it is my dearest wish that, one day, Bideford will see what they lost when they took the Mayor's chains away from Thomas Beale.

A hive of activity on the River Torridge

Chapter 8

The Merchant Ship Owner 1688

John Davie is one of the most successful local merchant ship owners trading with the colonies during the heyday of Bideford's success; the town has become an 'Abode of Opulence' and the importation of tobacco, the 'Lotus Leaf of Torridge', has made the town the second largest importer of the plant after London. Bideford is becoming ever more prosperous as it builds more and more ships and provides more and more supplies to meet the demands of both the market for tobacco and the needs of the new and flourishing colonies in Virginia and Maryland.

Extract from the Diary of John Davie –
Merchant Ship Owner of Bideford
in the County of Devon
Thursday August the 24th 1688
For my son Joseph and my daughters Henrietta and Anne

At last, my dear children, the remainder of our new home is ready for us to live in. I have named it Colonial House because of the debt I – and, ultimately, you – owe to those new towns in Virginia and Maryland that have made our life here in Bideford so comfortable. Now there is an hour or so before luncheon and time for me to preserve a few thoughts, so that you may always remember where your good fortune originated. These words to you form part of my journal which is a personal and private missive that you will not read until after my death, whenever God decides that will be. However, by recording and reflecting upon the blessings currently enjoyed by our family, this entry will become a small legacy to you all.

Though, of necessity, I have occupied this magnificent study for some weeks, today the carpenters are finally leaving it and, as I write, your mother is delighting herself with installing us into the remainder of it. And how grand it looks! I am particularly proud of the staircase and the splendid ceilings. To my eyes, it is every bit as imposing as the new houses being built in Bridgeland Street that everyone is talking about. Nay, more so. Personally, I find Mr. Gascoyne's architecture a little severe for my taste. But here we have a fine family house, one to which I shall look forward to returning, especially after the long voyages to Maryland and Chesapeake I must make from time to

John Davie walks towards Colonial House

time. I hope you all will be as proud as your father when your time comes to take charge of it yourselves.

You may wonder why I decided to have our house built on the east side of the Torridge. The answer is very simple. To be located so near to my bonding warehouses means I can conduct all my business from the eastern side of the Torridge without becoming embroiled in the maelstrom that has become the Quay. Each time the ships return from overseas it is all chaos and cacophony over there as they attempt to unload and store their cargoes on carts and truckle-mugs. It is so much calmer here. Fortunately, the biggest pottery, Mr. Beale's in Potter's Lane, has agreed to deliver his earthenware consignments direct to the ships. Mr. Yeo's pottery is also close by, as is that of Mr. Wilbraham and, therefore, it is easy to take delivery of their earthenware onto my ships. What a blessing!

Never a day goes by when I don't give thanks to that great Lord of the Manor, our own Sir Richard Grenville, for his brave exploits in the New World. In the 100 years since his voyages we, and many others beside, are reaping the benefits with a fullness of life and wealth that would have been previously unimaginable for a sleepy little Devon town like this.

And today Colonial House is complete. I cannot deny that I shall find it even harder to leave you, my dear children and, of course, your mother. Nevertheless, I must continue with my voyages and take advantage of the business I have strived so long and hard to build up for us all. You are too young yet to understand where I go and why I must leave you; and who knows how long it will continue, for these times cannot get better indefinitely. Who knows what the situation will be when you read this? It is my

Lunch in Colonial House

opinion that such prosperity cannot last indefinitely, as the new colonies find not only their feet but also their voices. It is only a matter of time before they will want the wealth they currently generate for others to remain with them. As memories of their original homes hereabouts grow ever dimmer, their loyalties will inevitably change. I fear we will have a fight on our hands at some point in the future to continue bringing the spoils back across the Atlantic.

For the record, then, I currently carry out my trading activities in Newfoundland, North Carolina, Maryland, the West Indies, Ireland, the Mediterranean and the Baltic. Why, you may ask, do I need to go myself to the American colonies? Well, from time to time, I need to ensure that my people there are content, especially now there is such competition from the likes of John Smith and George Buck who both sail from this town also.

My Master tells me the *Bideford Merchant* is almost ready to sail, so and I must leave once more on tomorrow afternoon's high tide. Her itinerary this time will be a straightforward one: first, to stop in Ireland with a consignment of earthenware and then to continue straight to Maryland with the remainder of the goods. By this time, the premium tobacco crop will be ready to load and then it is straight back across the Atlantic to Bideford before winter sets in. How I look forward to passing Christmas together in our new home!

Yesterday, the Master of the *Merchant* and I were able to take luncheon here for the first time, albeit in my study. We talked about the new American enterprise I have in mind for the shores of Chesapeake Bay – an enterprise I hope that you, Joseph, will play some part in when you are a little older. Indeed, when you read this, I pray that you, too, are able to sustain the family with its rewards. The Master is a good man and, unlike many, has no wish to invest his own money or have a share in the ships he commands. He knows I reward him well and he is content with that and displays unfailing loyalty. We agree that to build ships on the Chesapeake makes very good sense. Timber is cheap on those virgin shores. If we have ships on both sides of the ocean, we can double the amount of trade we conduct to and from Bideford. I am particularly concerned by the plans John Smith already has to build his ships on the banks of the Chester River in Chesapeake Bay.

We also talked about how many new families we would be taking as emigrants from Bideford on this voyage under the Headright system. I have seen you watching the families lining up on the Quay, surrounded by bundles of belongings. I often wonder if you know what they are doing. To pay £10 to start a new life on the other side of the Atlantic Ocean is an enormous leap of faith. I doubt very much that the system will operate for too much longer as the colonies become increasingly self-sufficient. But, at the moment, it is still proving popular. Apparently, they have been making their way in from the surrounding villages for days now, even sleeping on the Quay as they wait, anxious to find a ship willing to offer them a better life overseas. I can't say that I blame them, despite the town's new prosperity. Now that the colonies are well-supplied, there is not as much hardship as there was encountered by the earlier emigrants. Nevertheless, they still need more skilled men so that they cease to be dependent on England. Of course, this presents other problems in the long term, but for the present, it is an elegant solution. And, of course, the

The Bideford Merchant is loaded on the Torridge

people need to produce children to ensure the colonies' long-term survival.

But, my dears, back to the present. Make no mistake, this will not be an easy crossing. It is fraught with danger, especially this year with the weather so unsettled and unseasonal. There have been frequent sou'westerly gales of late and getting past the Lundy Road will be hazardous to say the least. There have already been many losses this year in that vicinity. I hear say that the merchantman *Dove* was so badly damaged by a storm south of Ireland she's had to turn back to Bideford for repairs. Her Master told me he knew there was no way she would get across the Atlantic like that and between Hartland and Lundy, it was so rough, he could not even be sure that she wouldn't break up completely, with the loss of all hands.

But enough of this morbid talk. It is almost the hour to pass some time with you all. I wonder what cook will provide for us today? A nice steak and kidney pudding, I hope. Your favourite too, Joseph! Then I shall go and check on the *Merchant*. It will be a long day tomorrow, our last in port, and I want to ensure I spend as much time as I can with you. I fear it will be many months before we can share our new home once more.

Until the day I die, until the day you read this, I will always be your loving father,

John Davie

Chapter 9
The Cod Fisherman
1720

When was the last time you were soaked to the skin? That's what I want to know. The last time you felt water running down your back into the waistband of your breeches? The last time your feet were that spongy and numb from weeks of never being dry, it was like having two dead fish at the end of your legs? When were you so cold and tired that you had to force yourself to put one foot in front of the other and everything was slowed down because you are fighting sleep? Have you ever forgotten what it's like to wash? Or forgotten the last time you slept in a bed with a mattress? When getting home at the end of the day is an impossible dream?

For me, Mattthew Prust, these things happen all the time. Every year, for months, it's like this. And today is the worst of all days.

It's getting on for seven months since I was last at home in Bideford. I left there in March and it took six weeks as usual to sail across the ocean to Newfoundland, weighed down with everything us need to make possible this year's cod fishing. The days get longer and longer then on the Grand Banks where us fish. Work goes on all hours rebuilding the quarters, our workshops, drying racks for the cod, landing stages, even our fishing boats and the barrels to keep the fish in once they're salted. The fish always get here towards the end of June. Then, there be no time for anything but dealing with they.

Anyway, now it's sometime in mid-October, I think. I'm not sure of the date or the day. It's all the same to me. Us can only tell how near us is to going home by where us is in the season and by the movement of the sun, the length of the days. And by the way I look and the way I smell. You see, by now, everything about me is black and greasy, my hair is stinking, slimy string. My face and teeth, my hands and fingernails are all solid with black fish dirt. All I can taste is cod oil. My coat and shirt, my breeches, my cap – all stiff with months of reeking filth. But it's my boots that are the worst. Fish oil and cod guts are rotting the seams now. It's enough to make the hardest man retch. Even I can barely stomach the heaving stench of it. On top of that, I haven't slept for two nights. Sometimes, I think I am not a human any more.

But I know I have to keep going because it's the last push. Because today is the last day here in the damp, cold fog of these Grand Banks for this year. Today, the *Exchange* will leave Newfoundland, bound first for Cadiz in Spain. The ship is heaving and laden with cod, all salted and stored in the barrels and the train oil from the cods' livers too, precious and valuable that is. Already I'm starting to dream just a little bit about feeling Spanish warmth in my bones. I keep saying to myself 'soon, Matthew, soon'. It keeps me alive, I swear it, to dream of washing myself clean, over and over, to wash my garments, to shave and dig that grime out of me, to scrub my feet in endless tubs of warm water, to melt the ice that has preserved my heart somehow through these last months. To eat and drink food fit for a human, not to look at a sea heaving with fish and, most of all, to look forward to the last leg of the voyage. When us leave Cadiz for Bideford us will be loaded up with wool, of course, along with some of our own train oil. But us will also have on board they beautiful fat lemons and figs, oil from olive tree fruit, nuts and wine. Things us never has in Bideford, the best the Mediterranean has to offer.

Many of the Bideford boys will already be home from the Banks, already working on the herring boats for winter. This year, all I want is to be back in time for Christmas with my Sally and my little ones. It will be a close-run thing. Ah, this final day in the Banks. Am I just dreaming about all these things? Lemons and such? Will I ever see Bideford again? Yes, I tell myself, over and over. Soon, boy, soon.

24th December 1720

Christmas Eve in Bideford! Made it just in time! Ha, I be a lucky boy and my Sally will be that pleased. Her don't know I'm back and it's my intention to surprise her. The *Exchange* dropped anchor just two hours ago, near the Long Bridge. I'm lucky to be on Uncle Tom's ship. He do take care of us the best he can. He promised us would be home and he kept his word. I heard tell there have been 28 ships in the Grand Banks and not all of them have arrived back for Christmas. 'Tis twilight now and I have just walked up from the Quay after us finished to find

Matthew Prust at the bottom of Cooper Street

Cooper Street full of laughter coming from the alehouses. There be plenty of boys already in there making merry. I am happy for them but I am happier to think of my family and my home awaiting me. I have something special for Sally. One of the Spaniards gave me some crystallized fruit to give to her. I can't wait to see her face! Mind you, the smell of ale and baccy is a bit of a temptation along with all they familiar Christmas songs out of tune. Even the bad odours make me smile. They'm all the smells of home! I am alive again – dry at last, clean as a new pin, close-shaved too. But my, I be so bone-tired and so relieved to be home, I can barely speak. And there be St. Mary's striking four. My tired eyes are filling up with tears It isn't the woodsmoke that's doing that …

"You'm back, then, Matthew. Did'ee 'ave a good catch, boy?" Constance Quicke! No mistaking that old voice.

"Fair enough this time, Mistress Quicke. Thank'ee. Happy Christmas to you and your family."

"And Happy Christmas to you and Sally, my lover. I'm sure 'twill be so. And they children will be plaised to see 'ee, I'll be bound. I've got a great big dish of brawn here for dinner tomorrow. Us always has it. Handsome 'tis. Just you look at that!" She lifts a cloth off the dish to show me.

I smile but can't raise the energy to carry on talking. She's seen it all before, boys so tired us can barely think straight.

"Listen to me nattering on! All you want to do is get on home. Cheerio then, boy. I'll be getting along."

I raise my hat and wave, carrying on up towards Mill Street. No more than a few steps later, I hear another familiar voice and see a staggering shadow in front of me.

"Well, I'll be jiggered! If it isn't Matthew Prust home for Christmas! How be 'ee, my boy?" Tommy Cox belches. "Ahhhhh … that's better."

"Hello, Tommy? How be you?"

"Hmm, tell 'ee the truth, boy, I been down the Bush Tavern since dinnertime and I was just takin' the long way 'ome to try and sober up a bit. My, 'tis a fine sight for sore eyes to see 'ee back yer." Tommy slings an arm around my shoulder. "Now, if you just care to help me back up the hill, for I got a little sway on, I believe."

I'd seen Tommy like this more times than I care to think of. I hold his arm around my shoulder and drag him on up the street "Come on, then, your Liza will be waiting for you."

"Oh yur, you can be sure of that. Her'll be there with a pan to hit me over the 'ead with, I fear!"

"I'll walk with 'ee so far as Mill Street. Jus' you hold on tight now."

"Yur, Matthew … 'ave I still got my shoes on?"

I look down at his feet.

"Yes, they'm both still there, Tommy."

"Then I can't be so bad. When I am the worse for ale, I 'ave been known to take they off and leave 'em on The Quay!"

I'd seen him do this before, too. And collecting them again the following day! I'm surrounded by people I've known all my life, the constant sounds and smells and sights of home. My heart pulls with it all. We stagger our way up towards Mill Street and, at the bottom of Gunstone, I stop. Tommy is quiet now, humming a little tune to himself, but barely conscious, dragging one foot after the other, arm still slung around my neck. I slap

Matthew and Tommy in Mill Street

him gently across his whiskery old face. "Come on now, Tommy. I've turned "ee towards home. Just you follow they feet straight back to Willett Street now. D'you hear?"

"You'm a good boy, Matthew Prust. Always was, even as a nipper. Yes, straight home for me, now. Happy Christmas, lad."

I watch for a moment to make sure Tommy's feet are heading home then I carry on up Gunstone. Almost there, Sally!

How lucky I am. Only 24 but I'm learning my trade well and already on the Newfoundland ships for four years. Good pay alright, but you need to know what you're doing to survive there. It's so hard, and I keep reminding myself that only the toughest fishermen and sailors can do it. That's why they call the Newfoundland Fisheries the Nursery of Seamen. Sail there, sail anywhere. That's what folk say around these parts. I'd like to get on one of the big baccy ships going to Maryland and Chesapeake and I know Sally would be happier if I was working for Mr. Davie or Mr. Smith or Mr. Buck. I would like to emigrate to the colonies, now they'm properly set up. A new life and new opportunities away from Bideford, but I'm not sure Sally would want to leave her family behind. I'm going to talk to her about it this Christmas. To me, it's a chance to be grabbed, but I'm an old hand now, sailing the Atlantic, used to all the dangers. It wouldn't be easy for Sally and they little tackers.

Ha! Blow me down if I'm not home already! My feet have brought me here without me having to think about it! And just look at how her have decorated it for the little ones. They love Christmas. Now where's that little box of sugary oranges? Ah, yer 'tis. Right, let's see her face! Oh my darlin' Sally, Christmas will be wonderful this year …

Matthew arrives home for Christmas

By Boxing Day, I have slept, eaten Sally's food and been constantly warm in my body and in my heart. Sally has cut my hair and tended to the calluses and splits on my skin. She loves the little sugary fruits I brought her. Now I am on the settle in front of the fire with Sally next to me, eating her fruits and the children at my feet.

"Tell us, faither, tell us what you do in Newfunland?" This year, Bertha and Daniel are old enough to hear for themselves what life is like for me when I am there.

"Well, my little beauties, 'tis like this yer ... "

I move further back into the old settle beside Sally and invite the children onto my knee. They snuggle in and the stories begin. First, I tell them about the storms that make the *Exchange* roll so badly that port and starboard decks hit the waves before she can right herself again. Then I hold them tight and tell them about the fog on the Grand Banks and the ghostly figures that rise up out of them, their hands and arms trying to curl themselves around me, black, gaping holes where eyes and mouths should be. The children shudder, their little eyes wide with concentration.

"Then, as us get near to St John's Bay, the shoals of cod are so thick that the boats can't move forward! Imagine that! Fish stopping a big old ship like Great Uncle Tom's *Exchange*!"

I tell them what it is like to start every year from nothing while us wait for the fish to arrive.

"But we're not all fishermen, you know, my beauties. There's all manner of jobs for they Bideford men who don't fish," I say.

"What jobs, faither?"

"Oh. Now, let me see. There's the splitters, the headers and the throat-cutters who chop off the cods' heads, split their bellies open, save the liver for th'oil, take out the guts and cut the fish up in pieces ready for the salters and the barrow men."

The children screw up their noses and put their fingers in their ears.

"But the real 'ard work's what I do," says I. "Off us goes ev'ry day in threes, in our little boats to catch they cod with our rods and lines. Long, long hours, wet, hungry and frozen in they tiny boats, catching cod. Shivering in the cold wind all the time, our fingers freezing in they woollen gloves your granny knitted for me. And the Grand Banks, mind, they fogs can hinder our journeys back and forth to shore somethin' awful. And if us drift out too far, us can't hear the fog horns and us may not get back at all. Ever!" I squeeze them hard and they laugh their beautiful laughs.

I tell them what it's like to be wet. Really, really wet. What it's like to feel like I felt when I started telling you this story. It makes me shiver even now, warm as I am, to think about having to go through it all again in less than four months. I must talk to Sally tomorrow about the baccy ships. The children are clinging on to me, holding me close, keeping me warm. Then they begin to tickle me and laugh and all those times are forgotten. This is why I do what I do and this is why I will continue to do it, if I have to, to keep my family safe and give them a future. It's a steady job, little prospect of stopping, so far as I can see. I hold on to the hope of something more, but for now it's enough to know there isn't a better fisherman than me in the whole of England. And that's the truth.

Chapter 10

The Dark Side
1752

Do you know the difference between a privateer and a pirate?

Pirates are ruthless and violent criminals who sail the high seas looking for, attacking and capturing other ships to steal their cargoes and treasure. Quite against the law. Pirates still operate today in many parts of the world.

Privateers operated in the 16th, 17th and 18th centuries. They were 'pirates with permission'. Privateers did the same things as pirates – the only difference was that they did it in the name of the king or the queen and so it was a lawful activity. Privateers were heroes. Pirates were villains. Bideford's Sir Richard Grenville was a privateer for Queen Elizabeth I and his ships, all armed, could also be used by the monarch in times of war. Remember the Spanish galleon *Santa Maria* that Sir Richard captured and brought back to Bideford? That was a ship he took as a privateer. You would not dare to call him a pirate! Privateering was the dark side of seafaring success and wealth. It was accepted by all.

The Dark Side

In the two centuries after Sir Richard Grenville's voyages of discovery, new trading opportunities shaped the Torridge communities, bathed them in the glory and light of success and prosperity. But with all that came another dark side. There was still filth and ignorance, cruelty and poverty, disease and death, hardships of all kinds and questionable activities existed in the effort to survive the harshness that lurked, often unseen, behind the prosperity enjoyed by others. Smuggling was commonplace and well organised by local folk, who knew the rugged coast of North Devon well. They lit beacons of fire on the cliffs to lure laden ships onto the granite teeth of rocky reefs that prevail here. And it was locals who, out of necessity, would board these stricken vessels to 'relieve' them of their valuable cargoes.

But in this final story, you will see how forces other than necessity fuelled that dark side – the forces of greed and the abuse of power. It is a story of a merchant trader from Northam, a successful and highly respected man. He had one of the largest shipping fleets on the Torridge and was trading in America for tobacco and in Newfoundland for cod, like many of his contemporaries. He was also a successful privateer for the crown against the Spanish. He had been High Sheriff of Devon and, in 1747, was elected the Member of Parliament for Barnstaple. He had helped the lives of many local families whose men worked on his ships. But he was a merchant guilty of a wicked crime. It was a crime that the Master of one of his ships paid the penalty for with his life and which, for the merchant, turned peoples' respect to hatred.

You can find Knapp House sitting a little way back from the road that runs between Northam and Appledore.

Thomas Benson as a child at Knapp House

It was here that Thomas Benson was born in 1707. As a child, he spent his days watching the river Torridge from his bedroom window or running down to the marshland at the bottom of his garden to watch the big trading ships sailing towards the Bar from Bideford; ships heading for Spain, Portugal, France or across the Atlantic to the tobacco colonies or to Newfoundland for cod. He would wander down to the Quay at Appledore and listen to the yarns told by sailors there and, from an early age, he dreamed of the day when he, too, would have a fleet of ships of his own.

By the time Thomas Benson was 40, he had fulfilled his dream and become one of the most successful and wealthy local merchant traders in the American colonies. But, despite all the work he had created for men along the Torridge and the respect he had earned from local people, Thomas Benson's renown and riches gradually turned him into a different man. A man who believed he could buy anything he wanted and make anyone do anything he wanted – as long as he paid enough. He became greedy and thought his riches gave him the right to ignore the law of the land.

The dark side began to take hold when he started cheating the authorities out of customs' duties he owed on tobacco he was importing. He had leased Lundy Island from some of his influential politician friends, where he began to drop off some cargoes of tobacco on his way back to Bideford. So when he sailed back home and the Excise men checked his cargo, surprised though they were, there sometimes simply wasn't enough tobacco in the hold to pay duty on. Thomas Benson had become a smuggler! And you can still find the cave on Lundy where he hid his smuggled tobacco.

Smuggling at Benson's Cave on Lundy Island
© *David Medcalf (photograph)*

The Dark Side

Not only that, but he had used his influence to get a government contract which paid him to take convicts to the colonies. The government used imprisoned men and women as labour to help with the hard work of turning the young colonies into places fit for the raising of families. But most of the convicts Thomas Benson was paid to deliver never reached America because, on the way and under his instructions, they were taken off his ships at Lundy where they worked for him as slaves, making improvements to the island. He sent just enough of them to America to get the signed piece of paper he needed to collect his fee, saying the others had died on the journey across the Atlantic.

But none of this was enough to pay his rising debts. By 1752, Thomas Benson owed the Customs authorities £8,229 – a huge amount of money, millions by today's value – and he knew that he would have to take drastic steps to clear the debt or face ruin. He began to make a Plan. It was highly dangerous, fraught with difficulties, heavily reliant on the co-operation of others and completely unlawful. But, by this time, the dark side had taken over the head and the heart of a desperate man. Of course, if he were found out, he would face death by hanging. Not only that, he was taking two very big risks. First, he needed to persuade the ship's Master to go along with The Plan. Second, he would have to keep the crew quiet.

So, what was The Plan? If they were sensible, merchant ship owners trading overseas had insurance to protect them in case something went wrong. If it did, the insurance company would pay the ship owner the value of whatever was lost or damaged – even the ship itself if it had foundered. Now, think about Thomas Benson's situation:

1) He owned ships that carried valuable cargoes and valuable convicts

2) He rented Lundy Island, just 15 miles out from where the voyages began – a remote, uninhabited lump of granite that no-one, except Thomas Benson and his friends, ever visited

3) Everything was insured

The Plan became clear to Thomas Benson and it would be executed on board his oldest brigantine, *The Nightingale*.

Captain John Lancey had been ship's Master on many of Thomas Benson's voyages. The Captain was a good man with a young family, very loyal to his employer and very honest. He was the only member of the company put together to sail *The Nightingale* personally asked by Thomas Benson to co-operate actively in The Plan. Captain Lancey was summoned to Knapp. When he arrived, Thomas Benson was standing at the window of his study, looking out over the fields towards the Torridge.

"Ah, Captain Lancey, good morning. Will you take a small drink with me, sir? I have something to discuss with you."

"No sir, thank you. I have much business to attend to before this voyage and I must be brief. May I ask why you have asked to see me? I thought my instructions were clear enough."

Thomas Benson paused a moment. "I'm afraid I have encountered some rather formidable problems, John."

"I'm sorry to hear that, sir."

"Yes, well, that's as may be. But you, John, are the only man who can help me out of this ... predicament."

"How so, sir?"

"The fact is, Captain, I owe a lot of money and it has reached the stage where I must take rather ... drastic action. I would not be talking to you like this if I were not desperate." Thomas Benson walked slowly from the window and back to his desk. "I have no choice but to scuttle *The Nightingale.*"

"But this is madness, Mr. Benson! No, sir. Absolutely not. I want no part of this ... you must find someone else to take charge. I have a young family to care for and we will both hang if this folly is uncovered!"

"Now listen, John. If I do not do this – if you do not assist me – my debts cannot be cleared. I will lose my ships, this house, everything. I will be a broken man, sir. And what do you think will happen to your family then, hmm? And all the men in Appledore who rely on my ships to keep them in work? You have no choice, sir, if life is to continue in a prosperous fashion."

"Even if I agreed, sir, how could this foolishness be achieved without raising suspicion?"

Thomas Benson told Captain Lancey every detail of The Plan, during which the Master paced the floor. When he had finished, Captain Lancey turned on his heel.

"Again, Mr. Benson, no. I refuse to be part of this. I would rather have no work at all than to become a criminal in this fashion."

Whilst Captain Lancey made his passionate refusal, Thomas Benson was writing at his desk.

"Perhaps this will change your mind?" Thomas Benson handed Captain Lancey the piece of paper on which he had been scribbling. "Your family will never want for anything again, John. I promise you that. They will prosper well for this one act of loyalty. I also promise you that, if anything should go awry, I will personally protect you from any blame. You have my word on that, sir. The word of a gentlemean." He held out his hand.

Captain Lancey walked to the same window as Thomas Benson had earlier done in their exchange. After some moments, he turned back and held out his hand in return.

"I do not like this, Mr. Benson. Not at all. But I will do it for you, sir, as an act of loyalty for the good you have done for us all. I must tell you, though, my heart is heavy."

"It will soon be finished, John. Soon enough."

And so the first part of The Plan had been put into place. But what about the rest of the crew, some 60 men in all? How could Thomas Benson and Captain Lancey be sure they would comply?

Appledore chandler Thomas Powe was one of Thomas Benson's close, but dubious, friends. Powe knew something was going on when he was asked to hire the crew for *The Nightingale*. He was asked to promise each crew member a generous sum of money to say nothing if anything 'happened' on the outward journey. Naturally all of the crew became suspicious that something bad was about to take place, but they signed up just the same. They needed the work and Christmas was coming. One of the crew that Thomas Powe hired was Bo's'un James Bather. Bather was very worried about this promise of money and, at first, refused to accept it. Only when Thomas Powe promised him more, did Bather agree.

On August the 3rd 1752, *The Nightingale* slipped out of Appledore on the full tide bound for Virginia and Maryland. She was laden with Spanish salt, locally made woollen clothes, Irish linen, pewter and boxes of cutlery.

Convicts (12 men and 3 women) had been counted and loaded onto a platform above the cargo hold. Supervising the loading himself, Thomas Benson asked one of the crew to hide "a tobacco hogshead of dry goods" from the Customs Inspectors. No one, except he and Captain Lancey, knew what that hogshead contained …

After two days, *The Nightingale* dropped anchor in the Lundy Road, a well-known and well-used sheltering place for ships against westerly gales. As night began to fall, the entire cargo, except the salt, was offloaded by small boats onto the island. It took two nights. The convicts saw nothing of this and remained unaware of what was happening. They thought the ship was sheltering from a gale.

The following day, *The Nightingale* set sail once again. After 50 miles, another ship was spotted. *The Charming Nancy* had crossed the Atlantic from Philadelphia and *The Nightingale* exchanged traditional greetings with her – a bottle of wine and the wonderful gift of a fresh cabbage. Everything was 'normal'. Once *The Charming Nancy* was on her way again, Captain Lancey ordered the mysterious hogshead aboard *The Nightingale* to be brought to him. Inside were little barrels of tar and other fire-making material. Captain Lancey ordered two of the crew to place the items throughout the hold and one of them was then ordered to make a hole in the bottom of the ship below the water line. A candle was thrown in to start a fire and the crew, under orders, began to make weak attempts to put it out. All the while, they thought about the promise of money that had been made to them before they left Appledore. The truth of what was happening was dawning.

Crew and convicts moved into the lifeboat as *The Nightingale* began to sink. The fire was spotted by the

The Nightingale is unloaded in the Lundy Road
© *David Medcalf (photograph)*

Captain of *The Charming Nancy* and another approaching ship, *The Endeavour*. Between them, they managed to rescue all hands and take them back to Clovelly, whilst *The Nightingale* continued her new voyage to the ocean bed. All had appeared to go to plan. *The Nightingale* was lost and all hands were safe.

The day after the sinking, Captain Lancey returned from Clovelly to Knapp House to face Thomas Benson.

"Captain Lancey, sir." Thomas Benson was not a happy man. He was pacing his study floor.

"Mr. Benson. 'Tis all done as you wished, sir." Captain Lancey was curt with him, unhappy with himself to have been a part of this disaster. "*The Nightingale* has perished. The crew and convicts have all survived. They be on their way to the notary in Bideford to sign the insurance affidavit forms. As you requested."

"Did every crew member attend?"

"To my knowledge, yes, sir."

"Damn it, man, all has gone too smooth. It is bound to raise suspicions with the authorities! With the insurers!"

"With due respect, sir, should you not have foreseen this before the event?"

Captain Lancey was worried about Thomas Benson's next moves and not reassured in the slightest by this meeting. "Good day, sir. I shall be away to my family." He turned on his heel and strode out, before Thomas Benson had further opportunity to vent his anxieties and anger.

Thomas Benson was right to be worried. One crew member did not go to the notary in Bideford. Instead, the bo's'un, James Bather, went to Barnstaple and got very drunk. When he was very drunk, he was very talkative and there were a lot of people in the alehouses who heard what had happened to *The Nightingale* and who wanted to get Bather's side of the story. When Bather was drunk, he was also very honest. The truth about what had happened on *The Nightingale*, just two days earlier, was no longer a secret. The trouble began.

James Bather's story reached Barnstaple merchant, Matthew Reeder. Mr. Reeder was a big rival of Thomas Benson. He called Bather to his office. "Now then Mr. Bather, what's all this I'm hearing about *The Nightingale*? Scuttled, was she? Is that what you are saying, sir? That's a big accusation. Are you sure it's not just the ale talking?"

"No, sir, Mr. Reeder. I swear to'ee, 'tis the truth. I was there, see. And I 'elped it to happen, so 'elp me God. What hevver be I 'gwain to do now. I've blabbed good and proper."

Mr. Reeder watched him, arms folded. Bather turned his cap round and round in his big hands, thinking of the trouble he would cause his family.

"'Twas the ale you see. I'm always the same with the ale. I tell's the truth an' it gits me into bother." Big salty tears started to drop onto his jersey.

"Now calm down, Mr. Bather," replied Mr. Reeder. "All is not lost. I have a notion that if you would only go to see Mr. Benson's insurance company in Exeter and tell them what you have told me, you would be welcomed most warmly. Why, I do believe they would offer you a reward for the information into the bargain."

Bather raised his red-rimmed eyes to look at Mr. Reeder.

"Look, I will help you. I don't like to see an honest man suffer for the likes of those who should be taking responsibility for this … disaster."

Mr. Reeder called for his clerk to make the necessary arrangements to send James Bather to Exeter.

"You'm right, sir. That is what I must do. I be an honest man. Tid'nt my fault, all this yur. I just wants to be rid of it … Thank 'ee, sir."

But Mr. Reeder was not a man of his word. Bather was not rewarded in Exeter. Instead, he was arrested for his part in the crime and sent to Southgate Prison.

Meanwhile, knowing nothing of this, Captain Lancey took ale with Thomas Powe in Appledore to discuss the situation.

"Now then, Powe. This is a terrible mess. I rue the day I let Mr. Benson talk me into it and now he is up there pacing the floor with worry. What was I *thinking* of? Are you absolutely sure you have guaranteed the crew's silence?"

"Don't worry, Cap'n. Each and ev'ry one of 'em hev signed th'affidavit in Bideford 'smorning sayin' that 'twas an unfortunate accident. They hev sworn, so there's no more to worry about. Mr. Benson'll see you'm safe. It'll all blow over in a few days. Just you see."

As Captain Lancey was returning home, he saw *The Nightingale's* first mate, John Lloyd, running towards him. He looked agitated.

"You'd better get into hiding, Cap'n Lancey, sir! I 'ev just seen a police constable of my acquaintance on the road up from Bideford. I asked him what he was about and he did tell me that the man with him was a bailiff from the Sheriff of Exeter. They was lookin' for someone and they means business, Cap'n, make no mistake."

"Don't worry, Mr. Lloyd. Some fraudster in trouble, I'll be bound. Nothing for us to worry about. All will be well, you'll see."

But John Lloyd's advice had been good. Before long, Captain Lancey was arrested. The bailiff also had a warrant

Captain Lancey and Thomas Powe in Appledore

to arrest the entire crew. Captain Lancey was first held in The Swan alehouse in Northam and, from there, word spread quickly. Several of the crew gave themselves up. The bailiff talked to Bideford Town Clerk and it was agreed that, because the crew had all signed the document to say the sinking was an accident, only four of them would be held. The four included James Bather, who was already in gaol in Exeter for his drunken revelations. The remaining crew were completely cleared.

So it was that Captain Lancey, first mate John Lloyd and the ship's young cook, John Sinnett, were rounded up.

The prisoners were held in gaol in Exeter as they waited for the case against them to be built. All conditions in gaol at this time were terrible – no regular food, no means of washing, no toilets, no light and prisoners were usually chained up. But, for poor John Sinnett, things were even worse. It had been his first voyage and the authorities knew from Bather's drunken ramblings that it was Sinnett's brother, Richard, who had been one of the two sailors ordered to set fire to *The Nightingale*. The terrified young cook was held alone and in irons in St Thomas Bridewell Gaol. The authorities hoped he would change his story and admit that the sinking had been deliberate. But the innocent John Sinnett could not imagine Captain Lancey or Mr. Benson capable of such a terrible crime.

Captain Lancey remained loyal to Thomas Benson, despite being told, when questioned, that he would be freed if he gave evidence against him. However, by now, there was already enough evidence to take the case to trial in London where both he and Lloyd were put in Marshalsea Prison along with Thomas Powe, who had also been arrested and charged for his part in the incident. John Sinnett was imprisoned in Newgate and James Bather in Poultry Compter.

The conditions in each prison were even worse than the one before. A mixture of smells came from the cells – tobacco, filthy feet, stinking shirts, fetid breath and foul-smelling bodies. The stench – worse than any sewer or abattoir – poisoned the air. There was no respite. Prisoners looked ill with long, rust-coloured beards and dressed in rags. Some of them wore woollen caps against the damp and cold, others covered their heads with the cut-off feet of old stockings. Some hovered round visitors like cannibals, ravenous enough, it seemed, to eat anything. It was a cruel fate for any man. More so for these innocent victims of another's greed.

After the case moved to London, Thomas Benson left Northam for London himself to offer money for the prisoners' release so that he could smuggle them out of the country before any of them had the chance in court to blame him. Meanwhile, charges against him for smuggling and unpaid debts were increasing. In the end, after trying three times to have the prisoners released, he gave up. His house in London was seized and orders were given to seize Knapp House to cover his debts. Cleverly, he managed to set up a trust that took over his maritime trading activities on his behalf. And then, a ruined man, he slipped quietly out of Devon and fled to Portugal.

At the trial, James Bather's story was finally supported by the other crew members. John Lloyd was found not guilty, as were Bather himself and John Sinnett. Thomas Powe was returned to gaol in Exeter, charged with assisting Thomas Benson in the crime.

Marshalsea Prison, London

Captain Lancey, however, was found guilty and sentenced to death. He never once complained or tried to blame Thomas Benson. He was hanged at Execution Dock in Wapping on June the 17th 1754, almost two years after the sinking of *The Nightingale*.

And Thomas Benson? He had friends and contacts in Portugal and was able to begin trading once again. When he heard of Captain Lancey's death, he was filled with shame and guilt. He also heard of the public's hatred for him and the moves to expel him from Portugal to answer for his actions back in England. He fled again to Spain. Luckily for him, war broke out again between England and France and there were more important things to worry about than Thomas Benson. He was able to return once more to Portugal where he lived until his death in 1772.

Some say that he made a secret journey back to Knapp House before he died, but it was never proved. The dark side had done its very worst. It caused the execution of a ship's Captain placed under intolerable pressure by one of the most successful merchant ship owners on the Torridge, whose reputation would be forever tarnished.

Acknowledgements

The greatest thanks are due to the following people. The seeds of this book were sown 35 years ago and it would not have been started or completed without any one of them. To those no longer here, I would like to say sorry that it took me so long to repay your faith in me: The Rev. Alan T. Fleetwood, Muriel Goaman, Alison Grant and Steve Clarke OBE. I wish you were here to read what you started. Mark Myers, Barry Hughes, Harry Juniper, Mark Horton and Kit Mayers unleashed my imagination through their love of and expertise in their subjects. David Medcalf generously allowed me to use his photographs of Lundy to recreate Thomas Benson's smuggling activities there. Without Lorna Howarth's unfailing support and professional help, I would never have succeeded in turning these stories into a book. She and The Write Factor are a real blessing for authors. I would like to thank Jane Whittaker for her consistent endorsement of my abilities and unflagging faith that I could finish this project against what often seemed like overwhelming obstacles. My gratitude goes to my graphic collaborators, Jilly Bentley and Sue Bond, for their continuous encouragement, generosity and creative ideas. And, finally but primarily, for John Moat who instilled in me, from the age of 13, the importance of storytelling.

Bibliography

Arscott, Major W. <u>Notes on Old Bideford and District</u>. Bideford: Gazette Printing Service, 1953.

Beara, John. <u>Appledore: Handmaid of the Sea</u>. Bideford: John Beara, undated.

Bidefordian, A. <u>Memoirs of the Grenvilles at Stowe</u>. Vol. 1. Bideford: Blight, Cole and Others, 1858.

Boyle, Vernon C. and Donald Payne. "<u>Bideford</u>." <u>Devon Harbours</u>. London: Christopher Johnson, 1952. 135–51.

Bushnell, G.H. <u>Sir Richard Grenville: The Turbulent Life and Career of the Hero of the Little "Revenge"</u>. London: George G. Harrap & Co. Ltd., 1936.

Cell, Gillian T. <u>English Enterprise in Newfoundland</u>. Toronto: University of Toronto Press, 1969.

Christie, Peter. <u>Exploring Bideford</u>. Oxford: Thematic Trails, 1989.

Cumming, W.P., R.A. Skelton and D.B. Quinn. <u>The Discovery of North America</u>. London: Elek, 1971.

Duffy, Michael, Stephen Fisher, Basil Greenhill Greenhill, David J. Starkey and Joyce Youings. <u>The New Maritime History</u>

of Devon: From Early Times to the Late Eighteenth Century. Vol. 1. London: Conway Maritime Press in Association with the University of Exeter, 1992.

—. New Maritime History of Devon: From the Late Eighteenth Century to the Present Day. Vol. 2. London: Conway Maritime Press in Association with the University of Exeter, 1994.

Duncan, Alexander G. The Long Bridge of Bideford and Bideford under the Restored Monarchy. Bideford: N/A, 1930. Reprinted from the Transactions of the Devonshire Association for the Advancement of Science, Literature and Art.

Farr, Graham. Shipbuilding in North Devon. Maritime Monographs and Reports. London: Trustees of the National Maritime Museum, 1976.

Fielder, Duncan. A History of Bideford. Chichester: Phillimore & Co. Ltd., 1985.

Goaman, Muriel. Old Bideford and District. Bristol: E.M. Cox and A.G. Cox, 1968.

Grant, Alison. "Breaking the Mould: North Devon Maritime Enterprise 1560–1640." Tudor and Stuart Devon: The Common Estate and Government. Ed. Todd Gray, Margery Rowe and Audrey Erskine. Exeter: University of Exeter Press, 1992. 119–40.

—. North Devon Pottery. Appledore: Edward Gaskell, 2005.

—. North Devon Pottery: The Seventeenth Century. Exeter: University of Exeter Press, 1983.

Grant, Alison and Peter Christie. The Book of Bideford. Limited Edition Number 315 ed. Buckingham: Barracuda Books Ltd, 1987.

Greenhill, Basil and Ann Giffard. Westcountrymen in Prince Edward's Isle. Newton Abbot: David & Charles, 1967.

Hakluyt, Richard. Hakluyt's Voyages: The Principal Voyages of the English Nation in 8 Volumes. Everyman's Library ed. Vol. 6. London: Dent, 1907.

Horton, Mark. "Jamestown 400 – How Devon Founded America." Appledore Book Festival. Northam, Bideford, 2007.

Hulton, Paul. "John White, Artist." North Carolina Museum of Art V. Numbers 3 and 4 (1965): 41.

Kingsley, Charles. Westward Ho! 1855. Library of Classics Edition ed. London: Collins, undated.

Lysons, Daniel and Samuel. 'Parishes: Bickton – Bridford', Magna Britannia: Volume 6: Devonshire (1822), pp. 47–69. 1822. Avail: http://www.britishhistory.ac.uk/report.aspx?compid=50569. 28 December 2007.

Markham, Clements Robert and John Hawkins, Richard Hawkins, William Hawkins. The Hawkins' Voyages:

> During the Reigns of Henry Viii, Queen Elizabeth, and James I.: Ayer Publishing, 1970.

Mayers, Kit. North East Passage to Muscovy. Stroud: Sutton Publishing Ltd, 2005.

MacInnes, C.M. The Early English Tobacco Trade. London: Kegan Paul, Trench, Trubner & Co., 1926.

Middleton, Richard. "England: The Elizabethan Prelude." Colonial America: A History, 1565–1776. 1992. 3rd ed. Oxford: Blackwell, 2002. 8–14.

Miller, Lee. Roanoke, Solving the Mystery of England's Lost Colony. London: Jonathan Cape, 2000.

Nix, Michael. "A Maritime History of the Ports of Bideford and Barnstaple 1786–1841." Doctoral Thesis. Leicester University, 1991.

Prowse, D.W. A History of Newfoundland from the English, Colonial, and Foreign Records. Amsterdam: Meridian Publishing, 1971.

Quinn, David B., ed. North American Discovery Circa 1000–1612. New York: Harper & Row, 1971.

—, ed. The Roanoke Voyages 1584–1590: Documents to Illustrate the English Voyages to North America under the Patent Granted to Walter Raleigh in 1584. Vol. 2. London: The Hakluyt Society, 1955.

—. Set Fair for Roanoke: Voyages and Colonies, 1584–1606. London: Univeristy of North Carolina Press, 1985.

Rogers, Inkerman. A Concise History of Bideford. Bideford: Gazette Office, 1938.

—. A Record of Wooden Sailing Ships and Warships Built in the Port of Bideford from the Year 1568 to 1938: With a Brief Account of the Shipbuilding Industry in the Town. Bideford: Bideford Gazette Printing Service, 1947.

—. Ships and Shipyards of Bideford, Devon, 1568 to 1938. Bideford: Inkerman Rogers, 1947.

Rogers, W.H. Notes on Bideford Vols 1–3. undated.

Rowse, A.L. The Expansion of Elizabethan England. 1955. Introduction by Michael Portillo. 2003 ed. Basingstoke: Palgrave Macmillan, 1955.

—. Sir Richard Grenville of the Revenge. 1963 Paperback ed. London: Jonathan Cape, 1937.

Schama, Simon. "Could I have multiple personality disorder?" The Daily Telegraph. ed. Elizabeth Grice. London, 28th July 2010.

Strong, H.W. Industries of North Devon. 1971 ed. Exeter: David & Charles Reprints, 1889.

Thomas, Stanley. The Nightingale Scandal: Lundy and North Devon in the 18th Century. Bideford: Gazette Printing Service, 1959.

Unknown. Tedrake's Guide to Bideford and North Devon. Bideford: Western Express, 1895.

Vaughan, Alden T. Transatlantic Encounters: American Indians in Britain, 1500–1776. Cambridge: Cambridge University Press, 2006.

Watkins, C. Malcolm. North Devon Pottery and Its Export to America in the 17th Century. Washington: Smithsonian Institute, 1960.

Watkins, John. An Essay Towards a History of Bideford in the County of Devon. 1792. Subscribers Edition 1993 ed. Bideford: Lazarus, 1792.

Whiting, Frank E. The Long Bridge of Bideford. Bideford: Frank Whiting, 1945.